FOLD

TOM CAMPBELL read history at Edinburgh University, and currently works in local government. He wrote *Fold*, his first novel, during one of the spiteful and needless organisational restructures that has so blighted the public sector over the last ten years. He lives in London, and is married with three sons.

FOLD

TOM CAMPBELL

B L O O M S B U R Y
LONDON · BERLIN · NEW YORK · SYDNEY

First published in Great Britain 2011

This paperback edition published 2012

Copyright © 2011 by Tom Campbell

The moral right of the author has been asserted

Bloomsbury Publishing, London, Berlin and New York

50 Bedford Square, London WC1B 3DP

A CIP catalogue record for this book is available from the British Library

ISBN 978 1 4088 2187 9
10 9 8 7 6 5 4 3 2 1

Typeset by Hewer Text UK Ltd, Edinburgh
Printed in Great Britain by Clays Ltd, plc

MIX
Paper from
responsible sources
FSC® C018072

www.bloomsbury.com/tomcampbell

To Ingrid

Round at Alan's – January

'Bet four pounds,' said Simon.

'Call the four,' said Vijay.

'OK, I'm happy with that,' said Doug.

'Call,' said Nick.

'Fold,' said Alan.

Nick looked down at the dwindling pile of chips in front of him. It was only three weeks into the new year but like the new century and so many other things, this one seemed to have got old very quickly. What had happened to all his resolutions and good intentions? True, he hadn't decided to play poker less or even to play it any differently, but he had certainly vowed that his luck would improve.

Although, actually, and this was all relative of course, he tended to do better at Alan's than anywhere else. Or at least, he didn't mind losing here as much. There were sound reasons for this. For one thing, if they were at Alan's place it meant that they couldn't be at Doug's. Though, if it came to that, he didn't really like any of their houses. His own, obviously, but Vijay's was problematic as well – it was almost as big as Doug's, and smelt a bit funny. Simon's was no good either. It was small and dingy, and he was an awful, ungenerous host, but for reasons to do with class it didn't seem to bother anyone else.

Alan's didn't have any such drawbacks. In fact, in some ways it was the perfect home – it didn't overawe and leave you feeling fucked off, but it wasn't too revolting either. It was a house like many others in Reading and Alan was like so many other people who lived here now, albeit sufficiently lacking in confidence to make him more appealing than most. It was a nothing-special kind of house, built between the wars, Nick supposed, for a large working-class family, and now inhabited by two professionals and their possessions. The interior design was uncontroversial and successful, with natural woollen carpets, glass coffee tables and stainless-steel lamps, and, of course, all their stuff was the highest quality, even Nick could tell that. Wireless audio speakers, flat-screen television, Scandinavian cooking appliances: all the things that Nick didn't want and couldn't afford. But that was OK. He might have a problem with other people because of the value of their homes and the attractiveness of their wives, their intellectual accomplishments and their annual income, but it hadn't yet got to the point where he disliked them solely on the basis of their household goods. Not yet. No, Alan's place was fine – in fact, it wasn't much bigger than his own, though of course in a better neighbourhood and without any of his errors of judgement.

Nick finished his glass of wine. How much had he lost so far? More than Alan, which meant more than anyone else, but it was probably best not to know with any great precision. The drinking helped with that of course, though it had brought other problems. One of which was that he could never remember what his cards were. There were only two of them; even after a bottle of wine it really shouldn't be that hard. He lifted them up from the table again: the two of clubs and the nine of diamonds – well, to be fair, they were pretty forgettable. But that could all change, it depended on what happened next. It depended on what he did with them.

Alan dealt the flop face-up on to the table. The nine of clubs, the king of diamonds and the seven of clubs. OK, so now he had a pair of nines at least. That was reasonable, enough to keep playing, but what were the others up to?

'Bet two pounds,' said Simon.

'Call,' said Vijay.

'Meet the two, and raise another three,' said Doug.

'Call,' said Nick.

'Fold,' said Simon.

'Call the three,' said Vijay.

It was only recently that Nick had experimented with getting drunk while playing poker. Four months ago, round at Vijay's, he had found himself a hundred pounds down in under an hour and had grumpily taken himself off to the lounge for a bit when he had had the striking, if not especially novel, idea of raiding Vijay's drinks cabinet by way of compensation. It was typical of Vijay that although he barely drank himself he had an impressive and expensive collection of spirits, proudly kept in an extravagant mahogany cabinet next to the slightly too-big-for-the-room television. In half an hour, and really without too much effort at all, Nick had managed to work his way through what he estimated to be twenty-five pounds' worth of brandy and malt whisky. It was all a bit hard on Vijay who hadn't actually won anything that evening himself, but, after all, it was poker night – whoever expected it to be fair?

When he returned to the table, the results had been stupendous. He had *felt* stupendous, with special, superhuman powers. He could split atoms with his teeth, bring down kingdoms and destroy capitalism. The cards in front of him fragmented into endless and beautiful mathematical iterations, while his senses were extraordinarily developed – he could hear the music of the stars and the sadness of Africa. At some point in the evening he also became clairvoyant. In an hour he had made good his losses, and by the end of the evening he was a hundred and fifty pounds up, his best performance ever – a hundred and seventy-five if you included Vijay's whisky.

But since then results had been less impressive. At Simon's the month after he played drunk throughout and lost one hundred and thirty pounds. At Doug's he turned up so drunk that he nearly wasn't allowed in, and then lost heavily – so much so, that that sod Vijay, probably still annoyed about the whisky, had announced to them all at the end of the evening that Nick had achieved a record loss. And now, more gently but still having had significantly more to drink than any of his companions, he was once again losing. OK, nothing dramatically bad yet, but steadily, efficiently, and besides, he thought grimly to himself, there were still two hours left to play.

Alan dealt the fourth card on to the table: the two of hearts. Well, that was better – two pairs, nines and twos, with one card still to come. And Simon was out now, that was good news as well. A good pot here, and this evening could still be turned round. Maybe it would be his year after all.

'Check,' said Vijay. A check – he was passing the chance to bet, and doubtless hoping that everyone would do the same. So clearly the two of hearts hadn't done him any good. But he was never going to get away with that, not with Doug at the table.

'Bet eight pounds,' said Doug.

'Call,' said Nick.

'Fold,' said Vijay.

Alan dealt the final card on to the table: the jack of clubs. So all he would have to play with was the two pairs, nothing more than that. Now was that a good hand or not? Despite the fact that he'd been playing for more than three years, he still wasn't sure. Doug was leering at him confidently and unkindly. OK, given what was showing on the table, the very biggest hands, the four of a kind and full house were impossible and no one had ever even seen a straight flush, but there were three clubs on the table, which meant he could easily have a club flush. There again, he could have the ten and the queen to fit with the nine, jack and king on the table to make the straight. Or he might have a pair hidden, matching a third card on the table for three of a kind. That was the problem with two pairs, it could be beaten in so many different ways. Or, and this was just as likely, he could be beaten by nothing at all.

'Bet thirty pounds,' said Doug.

Well, that was entirely predictable. What did that fucker have? Nothing, probably. And what was he going to do about it? Was he really going to let him steal the pot with nothing more than a big bluff and a stupid grin?

'OK, I'll see you for thirty.'

Doug laid down his cards. It turned out that he had nothing better than two pairs either, except that he held the king of spades and the seven of hearts. That was what happened when you had two fucking pairs. Well, at least he hadn't folded, at least he knew why he had lost, but Christ – that was an expensive way to get beaten.

Given the limitations of alcohol, he had thought about trying to buy some cocaine or cannabis or amphetamines or something. He wasn't sure what exactly – things were now so bad that he didn't know whether he needed something to make him stimulated and overconfident or relaxed and laidback. All he really knew was that he wanted something to make him good at poker without totally fucking him up. Did drugs like that exist? Is that what smart drugs were? He was at the outermost edges of his knowledge. He was friendly with enough of the younger teachers at work, in fact he was *only* friendly with the younger teachers, to probably get *something* illegal, but it didn't seem a credible solution. He was forty years old – it was hardly the age that one normally started getting into recreational drugs. It just wasn't sustainable, and anyway the last thing he could afford now was a drug addiction, what with all the money he was losing at fucking poker.

As far as Alan could tell, he wasn't like the others. He didn't love poker night like Doug or Vijay, he certainly didn't profit from it like Simon, and he didn't need it like Nick. No, he just hated it. Hated it in the same way that he had once hated relay races, French oral-examinations, school discos, Freshers' Week, university tutorials, job interviews and team-building exercises. Of course, it didn't help that he was totally shit at poker. Really terrible – as bad as Nick and possibly even worse than the others thought he was. And the others knew, he knew, that he was bad. That was, of course, partly *why* he was so bad.

What was especially disappointing about it was that Alan had always thought that he would make rather a good poker player. After all, he was good at maths and being good at maths was part of it. He'd been in the chess club at university, and had always enjoyed board games – surely that should count for something? He was quiet, difficult to read – perhaps even, he liked to think, enigmatic. He programmed computers for a living, and hardly anyone understood, or was even particularly interested, in what he did or said. You would have thought that had to be an advantage.

What's more he was Jewish, or at least his father had been. Weren't Jews meant to be good poker players? He may not have absorbed much Jewish culture, but he had at least soaked up enough anti-Semitism to know what they were like: crafty, clever with money, avaricious, ruthless. Why wasn't he any of these things? And surely, his personality too should have been built for poker? After all, and there wasn't much point trying to get around it, he'd always been a bit of a *squirt*. Not quite a *creep*, it wasn't as if he was disreputable or dishonest or anything, but he had always had a lack of courage, an inability to speak his mind when most needed, and, he suspected, a general weakness of character. These weren't the kinds of things that one normally associated with greatness, but they were all qualities he had assumed would make for a good poker player. But maybe it wasn't like that. Maybe, like so much else, all you needed to succeed in poker was bad manners, self-belief and a big dick.

It was eleven o'clock. They had an hour left. How much had he lost so far? Probably no more than sixty, it could be worse. Less than Nick anyway, if that was any kind of benchmark. Simon had already dealt the two hidden cards and Alan had the seven and the king of diamonds. Well, it was certainly playable, but that might not prove to be a good thing.

'Bet three pounds,' said Nick.

There was the usual pause while Vijay thought about things, and then: 'Call three pounds.'

'Call,' said Simon.

'Call,' said Alan.

'Not for me,' said Doug.

Doug dealt the flop – three shared cards dealt face-up on to the middle of the table, and which, all the books and experts said, should tell you if this was a hand worth playing or not. Except that, as was so often the case, Alan still didn't know. There was a seven of clubs, a jack of hearts and a five of hearts on the table. So he had a pair of sevens. Now was that a good hand or not? In large part it depended if the others thought it was. The problem of course was that they would only think it was if he thought it was. But he didn't know what to think.

'Four pounds,' said Nick.

Now it was Vijay again, and Alan knew that this would take a while. Vijay's great strength was his thoroughness. He would invariably come up with the right answer, or something approximating to it, but it would take him a while to get there. He wasn't like Simon, who was unnervingly brisk with his decisions and bets, impatiently raising large sums of money as if he just wanted to get it over with and win as quickly as possible, which was usually what happened. And he wasn't like Nick, who did much the same as Simon but lost a fortune. No, Vijay liked to think things through and was impressively unconcerned about anyone else having to wait for him.

Thirty seconds, maybe even a minute, but at last Vijay had made up his mind. 'No, I'm going to fold this one.'

'Call four,' said Simon, without a moment's pause.

Well, it was good news that Vijay was out, because he never stayed in unless he had something worth playing. For the time being, it was probably safe to carry on, even if Simon seemed so upbeat. With a nod of the head, he threw his chips into the pot.

Alan didn't enjoy playing at home. He wasn't a natural host – not like Vijay or Doug. He had learnt somewhere, from one of the self-help books that he had been reading for most of his adult life, that there are two personality types – host and guest, and that correctly identifying which you were was critical to your prospects for professional and personal success. The accompanying questionnaire that Alan completed had made it abundantly clear which camp he was in. Did he enjoy being the centre of attention? No. Was he comfortable making decisions on behalf of others? No. Did he like taking responsibility for a group? No, he did not. The problem was, he wasn't much of a guest either. He'd never been one of life's entertainers, he didn't have a stock of amusing or outrageous anecdotes, he wasn't brave enough to make jokes, his political views were unformed and tended to change depending on who he was with, he knew nothing about sport and outside of computing he rarely felt confident enough to give an opinion on whatever was being talked about – and no one, apart from Vijay, ever talked about computers.

What he *was* was incredibly well behaved. He might not turn up beaming with good cheer and brilliant conversation, but he did turn up on time, and at least he was sober and remembered what people's wives were called. That was more than could be said for some people – Nick, for instance. He looked warily over at him now, careful not to catch his eye. He looked dangerously drunk.

Doug dealt the fourth card on to the table – the three of hearts. Well, that wouldn't do him any good at all. Plus, there were now three hearts showing, with one more card still to come, which meant that there was every chance that one of the others would be able to make a flush hand with five hearts.

'Bet two pounds,' said Nick.

'Meet your two and raise another eight,' said Simon, throwing his chips into the pot without a moment's hesitation.

One of the management consultants who mysteriously turned up at Alan's work every three months or so once told Alan that he suffered from a lack of confidence. At the time he had accepted this judgement without protest – after all, that's what unconfident people did. But he'd subsequently thought about it and he didn't believe that now. No, the problem wasn't that he lacked confidence, but that everyone else had *too much* of it. The whole world was suffering from a crisis of overconfidence. Nuclear physicists wrote equations on blackboards, confident that they knew how to destroy the planet a thousand times over. Jews and Muslims and Hindus and Christians went around killing one another, confident that they'd made the right metaphysical selections. And across the table Simon incautiously made his bets, confident not that he had the best hand, but that he would win. The problem was, he usually did.

But the more immediate problem was that it was his turn to bet. He could have done with a bit more time. Why was Simon betting so forcefully? Did he have a good hand, did he think he was going to make a good hand, or was it just that he *was* forceful? Was he sitting on two pairs, was he looking to make the flush? Or did he have nothing? Was he just, yet again, going to bluff and bully them out?

'Call ten pounds,' said Alan.

Alan looked closely at Nick, who was looking at Simon glumly. One of Nick's handicaps as a poker player was that it was always completely obvious what he was feeling. Of course, nobody knew what he was *thinking*. No one, probably not Nick himself or even Simon, could tell what kind of eccentric strategy or hare-brained analysis he was bringing to the game, but they could all see how unhappy or cross or disappointed or, sometimes, less often, pleased he was. He might not be all man, but he was at least all mammal – a warm-tempered, over-responsive, highly emotional beast. Maybe that was why Alan liked him more than any of the others. Or maybe it was because he was so bad at cards.

'Fold,' said Nick. Clearly he had been hoping to get through this round of betting as cheaply as possible, but had been driven out. So it would just be Simon and him left at the end. Well, he'd been here before.

Doug dealt the fifth and final card face-up on to the table. It was the seven of spades. That changed things. Maybe this wasn't hopeless after all – it wasn't another heart, for one thing, but it also meant he now had three sevens, three of a kind, and that was actually a pretty good hand. Wasn't it?

It was Simon to bet, and again he did so with authority and speed, as if he was already thinking about the next round, and just wanted to wrap this one up.

'Twenty pounds,' he said.

And so, inevitably, it had come to this. He had three sevens. There was seventy pounds on the table, and despite all the bets and cards and signals and information they had given one another, he still didn't know what he should do. Did Simon have the flush or not? It wasn't as if he didn't know him – they had been doing this every month for three years now. Shouldn't he be able to read and understand Simon in the same way that he could computer manuals, or Nick?

'OK, I'll see you for twenty.'

Simon turned over his hidden cards. Sure enough, it seemed that Alan had completely misunderstood the situation, because Simon actually had a straight. He had the four of diamonds and the six of spades hidden which, with the three, five and seven on the table, gave him a well-concealed run. Vijay sighed in admiration, and Nick shook his head looking sad, as Simon pulled the winnings towards him. And Alan, because he was Alan, congratulated him.

Of course, he shouldn't even have been at the table tonight, and not just because it would have meant that he wasn't getting beaten. What he should actually have been doing was trying to get Alice pregnant. It was a Friday evening. It was four days before ovulation. She was thirty-eight years old. She was fertile – at least all the doctors and tests said so. And what was she doing right now? She was upstairs in bed reading a book about babies, keeping out of their way, feeling fraught, forgotten and unhappy, and what was he doing? He was downstairs, in the kitchen, getting destroyed at cards.

Alan had come to suspect that there was some kind of opaque but sinister connection between his failure to win at poker and his failure to get Alice pregnant, but he wasn't sure precisely what. Not only was he hazy about the causal mechanism, he wasn't even sure about the causal *relationship*. Was he shit at poker because he couldn't get her pregnant, was that the problem? All men are childish until they have a child, isn't that what they said? Well, in that case no wonder he couldn't beat anyone at cards – whatever else it might be, poker wasn't a game for children. Doug and Simon and Vijay – they weren't children. Not even Nick was childish, though you'd probably hesitate to say he was a grown-up. This was a game in which the winners were tough; they had mental strength, a ruthless streak and the courage to hurt each other. Alan was forty-one years old, but for some reason he had never picked up any of these things.

Or was it the other way round? Was it because of his problems at the poker table that he couldn't get his endocrine-hormonal system to produce sufficient quantities of whatever it was he needed? It couldn't be ruled out. As all the doctors, specialist consultants, textbooks, DVDs and websites had told them, these things were very often psychosomatic – which meant that his stress levels and pointless anxieties and hopelessness were all inhibiting his biochemical functionality. Which meant, essentially, that it was his fault.

So all he could say with any confidence was that if he could sort out what happened at cards, then there was every chance that the rest would follow. He wasn't like Simon or Doug – he didn't want to win big, he didn't want to make money and he didn't want to humiliate anyone. He didn't even want to win consistently – he wasn't especially comfortable with taking someone's money month after month, with making someone else feel like he did. No – all he really wanted was not to lose, to sit at the table with other men who lived in Reading and were approximately his age and social class, to break even at cards, have a few drinks, moan about work and feel that he wasn't a sucker. There now, that really wasn't too much to ask, was it?

Lucky in cards, unlucky in love. Or was it *Unlucky in cards, lucky in love*? Nick wasn't sure. He'd never thought about it before. Either way, he could see its appeal. It appealed to him for one thing – one of those sayings that bolstered mankind's sense of cosmic justice and upheld the traditional Western duality of the spiritual and the material realms. Surely no one, by any rights, ought to triumph at both romance and gambling?

Looking around, he did a quick survey. Well, there was no doubt that Alan had got lucky, though you'd have probably said that whoever he'd ended up with. What's her name, Alice, wasn't terribly pretty, in fact not much better-looking than Alan, and she ought to do something about those glasses, but she was obviously all the things that don't seem important when you're choosing a life partner and then turn out to be completely vital. To begin with, she was outgoing and friendly, which was more than could be said for Alan. Or Janet, for that matter. She was clever and actually quite funny in a surprising sort of way, and had a job that he didn't understand but sounded like it was well paid. No – she might not be the complete package, but she was as much as anyone could reasonably expect. In fact, it was a mark of how good she was, and also probably how plain, that Nick didn't even feel bitter about her being with Alan.

There was Vijay – middling in cards and, well, middling in love. OK, she might be a great cook, but no one would really call him fortunate to be married to Sarita. Cultural relativism could only stretch so far, surely. Formidable was the euphemism. One of those sombre Indian women who must have reached a certain stage early on in life and then stopped getting any wiser or older, just bigger, and whose common sense and robust moral outlook had hardened into grumpiness. Not that Vijay seemed to mind. He had three children, two of whom were disturbingly overweight, and he didn't seem to mind about that either.

Simon was single, as far as anyone knew. But was he unlucky in love? As always with Simon it was impossible to tell. No wonder he thumped them at poker every month – that tricky bastard could be anything. He might have a string of mistresses, he might have some improbable and disgusting fetish, he could be celibate, could be gay, could be anything. Or maybe he was just lonely.

And then there was Nick himself. Was he lucky? Well, yes and no. Janet was not the kind of woman he had always dreamt of ending up with, he knew that even when he was getting married to her, and her qualities were of the durable kind rather than the spectacular, but he was hardly in a position to complain – after all, it wasn't as if she had exactly hit the jackpot. She was reasonably thoughtful, she had good life skills, her decisions were more often right than wrong, and she hated wasting money. No children, of course – she'd never been able to, but that was OK. It had been a blow, no doubt about it, but they'd long ago managed to skilfully rationalise their disappointment away, and it did mean that he'd avoided ever having to endure the profound developmental leap, not to mention financial trauma, of raising a child in the twenty-first century. All in all, it could be a lot worse.

And Doug? Well, there you go – Doug crassly disproved the rule, just like he ruined everything else. For Doug was lucky in cards, that was obvious, and equally incontrovertibly, gallingly, he'd lucked out with the wife as well. She was not in the least bit how Nick had imagined. He had of course been happily expecting the worst kind of Southern English disaster. A stringy, small-mouthed blonde nag, with a permanently unfriendly face and an addiction to out-of-town shopping and eating Caesar salads at Pizza Express, or perhaps, even more hopefully, one of those dismal burst tyres, whose top-heavy, big-lipped prettiness had, over the course of her thirties, collapsed into a stupendous, short-necked blob. Even if she had been a stunningly attractive twenty-five-year-old sex object, that would have been OK, that would have been recoverable – it would at least have been ridiculous.

But she wasn't any of those things – she was fucking Greek for starters. She was small, really tiny when compared with Doug, and she looked like a pretty little freshwater bird, with a polished bob of gleaming black hair, fine hands and nice, neat little gestures. And she wasn't called Linda or Michelle or even, let's be honest, Janet, but *Sophia*. Nor was she stupidly young. In fact, as Doug proudly let slip one night, she was actually, ever so slightly, older than him. Who would have thought it? Doug McLain – sophisticated and classy enough to have an older wife. More than that, sophisticated and classy enough to *know* that it was classy. Christ, it was all so depressing. As if he didn't have enough to be fucking depressed about. As if the poker wasn't enough.

It was the end of the evening. Alan had packed away his chips and handed out the money. They had all dutifully declared their results to Vijay, who was tapping them into spreadsheets on his little hand-held computer. It had been another wretched evening. Nick now lied to Vijay so often that he had stopped believing what the others said as well. In any case, it was a waste of time – everyone knew what had happened. It was the same every month – Simon and Doug would have done well,

Vijay reasonably OK, Alan would have got fucked, and Nick would have got *really* fucked.

Nick didn't mind Simon. No, he probably wouldn't ever like him, but he didn't mind him so much either. At least he was clever – a lecturer, which was sort of a teacher really or at any rate as badly paid as one, and anyway his house was small. Vijay, with his careful monitoring and gradual accumulation of wealth, was non-problematic, though he could do with taking a big hit one evening soon, just to be sure, and Alan – well, that poor sod lost almost as much as he did. No, the real issue was Doug. Despite the fact that they had been playing for three years, Nick still wasn't sure if Doug was more or less stupid than he looked. That was partly because he looked so stupid, with his great blunt nose, wet eyes and goofy hair. What did he look *like*? Like a full-English cooked breakfast; like his beloved, and fucking irritating, pet retriever; like a pub landlord in a low-budget television drama who used to be a professional footballer; like a sports instructor who ran a local chain of highly profitable fitness centres, which was exactly what he was.

Looking across at Doug now, as he re-counted his winnings, Nick could feel something important stirring inside him. A sense not just of moral despair but moral energy, a deep need for vengeance, even if he wasn't entirely sure what it was that he needed to avenge. All he could say for certain was that he had to do *something*. He had turned forty last month, that probably had a lot to do with it, and he'd also had too much to drink tonight, but it couldn't be just that. For the last few weeks now, there had been a squall of imprecise but power-ful thoughts that kept coming back to Doug. Whatever other phantoms and monsters he'd hyper-visualised over the years, he hadn't made Doug up. Doug was real. OK, he wasn't necessarily the cause, but he also wasn't simply a symbol for everything that had gone wrong and needed fixing, by which he meant breaking. But what was he going to do about it? Not very much probably – after all, it wasn't as if he didn't have enough to worry about. There again, it wasn't as if he had much else to do.

Round at Doug's – February

'So who's going to play with me for just two little pounds?' said Doug.

Alan grimaced and looked around for someone to exchange glances with, but no one saw him. In poker you can *fold*, you can *check*, you can *call*, you can *raise*. Hence, all you need is four words and some numbers to play the game. So why did Doug insist on using so many others? He didn't simply fold, he always had to say *It's got a little too rich for me* or *I'm going to stop playing with you gents*; he didn't call, he would *go along with that* or *meet that bet any time* or be *absolutely fine with that* and, most irritating of all, he didn't raise, he *turned the temperature up a notch*, he *put his foot on the gas a little* or he *made it a game for grown-ups*. What was his problem, what was wrong with betting the way you were supposed to, and, perhaps more to the point, what was Alan's problem? Why on earth did it bother him so much?

Alan had never claimed to have a highly developed aesthetic sensibility, but he had always had an appreciation for the simplicity of poker's signalling system. It was one of the things that had initially attracted him to the game, before it got ruined by the other players and getting beaten all the time. It was probably the computer scientist in him. After all, every computer program in the world was built upon such signals – whether one of his financial-modelling applications or a satellite-control system, it was nothing more than an elaborate and vast construction of logic gates. *Fold, call, raise.* NOT, AND, OR. Also, and again any good software designer would approve, the words were so impressively compact. *Fold* – it was so dense, so packed with information and meaning: prudence, retreat, defeat, loss, cowardice, financial ruin, humiliation. All compressed into just four letters. And then Doug comes along and wrecks it all with a *No way, José*.

Alan never felt comfortable at Doug's place – partly just because it was Doug's, but for other reasons – though he struggled to say what they were. Simon could probably describe them, or Nick, but Alan was less good at that kind of thing. Still, even if he didn't know why, he certainly knew *what* he disliked: the imposing white pillars on either side of the black-iron gateway, the ornate umbrella stand in the hallway, the framed portrait of Doug, his wife, two children and golden retriever, the slight echo in the enormous, chilly dining room. Was it vulgar? Did Doug lack good taste? Alan didn't feel confident enough about decorative art or the English class system to be sure, but he certainly hoped so.

'Your two little pounds, and I'll raise five pounds,' said Vijay.

'Fold,' said Alan.

'Fold,' said Simon.

'Call,' said Nick. 'And raise another one.'

Doug looked carefully at Vijay. Vijay was a terrible bluffer. Someone had once told him that Africans and Indians made for good liars because they had dark skins. And it was certainly true that Vijay didn't blush. Not like Alan, whose neck splotched and splashed salmon pink every time he tried to even slightly overplay his hand, though nowadays Alan went pink so often that it was practically his normal state, and no longer a reliable indicator of anything other than a general uselessness. No, Vijay didn't blush. But there were plenty of other ways that he gave the game away. Take what he was doing now, for instance – twitching and rubbing his fingertips together and puckering his lips like a naughty child.

So Vijay was bluffing. But what was that wanker Nick up to? One of the odd things about Nick was that, even though he was down at the end of every night, he always managed to do it in a different way. Some nights he was spineless, worse than Alan, and frittered his chips away with small loser bets round after round, always ducking out the minute it got tasty. Other nights he played like a maniac, wildly raising, bragging, betting like it was toy money. Sometimes he was as straight as anything, other nights he did nothing but bluff. It seemed the only thing that he did with any consistency was lose. It didn't help that he was off his head half the time. Pissed normally, the idiot, but more than once recently Doug had started to suspect he was on something else. It would be just like Nick to start taking drugs at the age of forty, ten years after everyone else had stopped.

In a way, Doug found it harder to play against him than anyone else, even Simon. For instance, what was he doing now? What kind of a half-witted play was that? Why raise on Vijay's bid? Or at least, why raise by a pound? What kind of bluff was that? Was it a bluff? For some time now, Doug had had a strange but nagging fear. What if it was actually Nick who was the best poker player among them? That the reason why Nick confused him, why his bidding was so erratic and his losses so substantial, was not because he was an imbecile but because none of them understood what he was doing. He was playing at a completely different level, which, one day, they would hazily grasp, and at which point they would immediately start to get heavily beaten. It was nonsense of course. Doug knew that. But it hadn't stopped him devising an elaborate fantasy in which he travelled with Nick to the World Series Poker Championships in Las Vegas, crashed out in the first round and then watched in horror as Nick, playing at last among his true peers, was crowned champion.

'I can live with six pounds,' said Doug.

'Call,' said Vijay.

And Nick, like the bloody idiot he was, folded. So this was Doug's for the taking. The last card came down, but Doug barely looked at it – this wasn't about the cards any more. Vijay was bluffing – it wasn't like him as a rule, but he was. Just to be certain, Doug decided to wait it out a bit, to let him fidget just a little bit more, making it clearer and clearer not just to Doug but to everyone round the table. And then, 'Raise ten pounds.'

He was pulling the pot towards him almost before Vijay had dropped his cards.

So – there we go, one hour in, and he was already forty pounds up. Doug liked playing at home. Vijay's spreadsheets simply confirmed what he had always known – that, even by his standards, he tended to perform well here. McLain Towers, as the others called it – but only half ironically. There was something else in their little joke, an acknowledgement of not just his pretensions, or what he aspired to, but also what he had. He had a very large house in a very nice street, and it was worth a lot more than most people's – a lot more than any of theirs. And on any number of scores, except perhaps cooking, he also had the best wife.

He looked across at his companions fondly. Doug loved poker night. It wasn't just the fact that he won so often, though that had to be part of it. There were many elements to it. For one thing, he liked his friends. Anxious Alan, chubby

Vijay, clever Simon. Even Nick. They weren't like his other friends – they weren't business associates, they didn't owe him anything, they didn't ask for things, they weren't related to his wife, they didn't come from Fife, they didn't know anything about sport and they didn't know who his brother was. All right, perhaps they weren't the most exciting company. No one would describe Alan as a brilliant laugh or anything and you wouldn't want to be on a stag night or at the rugby with them, but that was OK – he even liked that about them, and anyway he had stopped going to those kinds of things. He was forty-four years old and it was time that he had friends like this. It was, he couldn't help but feel, a highly positive development. These were exactly the kind of people who should be coming round to his house – a nice group of middle-class companions who were significantly less well off than he was.

They had boring jobs and when they weren't playing poker they talked about boring things which he was happy to give his views on and learn about: interest-rate changes, financial services products, innovations in car design and the quality of local public services. He liked it that they listened to his opinions. He liked it that their conversations were so useful. He had changed all of his life-insurance policies on the basis of a series of detailed conversations with Vijay, when he had bought new computers for work it was after careful consultation with Alan. It was Simon who instructed him on his wine-buying holidays in the South of France. Even Nick had been useful, for it was the realisation that his children would be going to the secondary school where he taught that had finally persuaded Doug to educate them privately.

This was what it was all meant to be about. It was why people wanted to live in places like Reading, and why people from places like Reading prospered more than people from Dundee, Kinross or Kirkcaldy. It was because the people were nicer to each other. They helped one another out with advice, consumer tips and good deeds, instead of just asking for stuff all the time and fucking each other up.

'Five pounds,' said Simon.

There was a little appreciative whistle. They hadn't even had the flop yet. What was Simon holding? A pair of aces? As Nick had expensively learnt over the last two years, even the strongest of hidden cards didn't count for much until they had seen what was on the table. More likely, Simon didn't have anything, but just wanted to fuck them up a little bit.

Much to Nick's irritation, Doug insisted on calling Simon *Prof*, as if he was the only one of them who had ever read a fucking book in his life. Naturally, Nick had done his research and had satisfied himself that Simon was a long way from being a professor. He was, in fact, a lecturer – and not even a senior one. Which meant, *Doug*, that he was at least two promotions away. Nor did he seem to be getting there at any great lick. Nick had gone through Simon's publications list and they were nothing to get overanxious about. A handful of journal articles that looked pretty much unreadable about cognition and language and some chapters for a book with a long, drab title published by Dundee University Press, and which Amazon couldn't promise to deliver for at least six weeks. What's more, his employment record was far from awesome – an undergraduate degree from one of the Northern universities, Nick couldn't remember which, followed by a doctorate and what sounded like a lot of dicking around in London, some work with the Open University, two years at the University of Buckingham, whatever that was, and now here in Reading. So much for the *Prof*.

What *was* problematic was that Simon was a lecturer in philosophy. With so few opportunities to feel superior, Nick had decided at quite an early stage in his life to be snobbish about the arts. He had then gone on to discover that mathematics, particularly if it was non-applied, was also an intellectual endeavour that should be respected, and that (some) of the sciences could also be OK as well: theoretical physics – yes; mechanical engineering – no; biology – maybe. He was sure that psychology could be safely written off as pseudo-science, and he knew that anything with the prefix *social* should be detested. But according to these same rules, which he only dimly understood but closely adhered to, philosophy had to be treated with a high degree of deference. It was ancient. It was abstract and devoid of any practical value. Upper-class people did it, and it was really difficult.

Nick himself had dropped out of Oxford. Twenty years later it was still his proudest achievement, the fact that he most quickly and casually tried to let slip on those increasingly infrequent occasions when he met someone he thought might be worth showing off to. True, he hadn't been *thrown* out of Oxford for insurrection or anything and the reasons why he left had seemed less impressive at the time – he was lonely and kept coming bottom in the exams – but at least he had rejected them, just, rather than the other way round. He had been given a place by a seventeenth-century college attended by two British Prime Ministers, three Chancellors of the Exchequer and a Poet Laureate, and he had made the heroic, maybe even existentialist, choice to leave.

'Fold,' said Vijay.

'Sorry, boys, I just don't fancy it this time either,' said Doug.

'Call,' said Alan.

Nick had the nine and ten of hearts. Well, that was easy enough – even for five pounds, even with just two cards, he had to stay in with a hand like that. But with Simon betting like this, it would, he knew, soon become more difficult.

'Call five pounds,' said Nick.

Although far and away the greatest thing he had ever done, dropping out had of course been a disaster. For one thing, it ended his relationship with his father, which meant that the relationship with the rest of his family never recovered either. It wasn't really a surprise. While getting out of Oxford had been Nick's biggest triumph, for his father it had been him getting in. It was, Nick supposed, the kind of story that a generation of post-war British writers made the basis for their dreary coming-of-age novels.

Now he knew why – it seemed that being estranged from your family *was* dreary, and also bloody hard work. At least, it was if you were stuck in the English lower-middle class, whose dreariness was its defining characteristic. If the Williams had been different, if they had been a highly entertaining family of metropolitan Jewish intellectuals, then they could have had sophisticated but emotionally charged disagreements and outlandish scenes in glamorous restaurants. If they had been delinquent Irish Catholics living on a social-housing project in Liverpool, then they could have had spectacular drunken punch-ups. At least that way it could have all been resolved quickly. But no – Nick's father was a tax officer and they had lived in one of the quieter parts of Peterborough, and apart from some Welsh cousins, there was nothing in the least bit exotic about them. And instead of being settled in one act of grand theatre, it was a long, drawn-out affair, an attritional conflict lasting years, made up of guarded Christmas dinners, tense birthday celebrations, and difficult, hurtful conversations in the car whenever his father picked him up from the train station. There wasn't even a proper reconciliation, just a hastily patched up return to dignified behaviour and some unconvincing attempts at intimacy in the two months between his father being diagnosed with cancer of the bowel and dying.

Down came the flop: the four of spades, the jack of spades and the three of hearts. This gave him something to think about. It still had plenty of potential – the nine, ten and jack was promising, and he had three hearts as well, but Simon, that fucker, was quite needlessly going to make it expensive for him to take this anywhere.

'Eight pounds,' said Simon.

'Fold,' said Alan.

Nick raised his face from the table. He didn't want to look at the cards and most of all he didn't wanted to look at the other players. His eyes searched out and rested upon a silver-framed photograph on the mantelpiece. It was a picture he knew well, a black-and-white portrait of Doug's wife Sophia, but on her own for once, without her ghoulish family around her. It was also only in this photograph that he ever saw her sitting still, instead of striding across the house, her head turned to one side, majestically ignoring them. He had studied it many times over the years, but to no great effect. Basic questions remained: who took it and where? Why didn't she smile like that now? Her hair was longer and instead of being pinned back it fell untidily down to her shoulders – why didn't she wear it like that any more? It had obviously been taken some years ago; maybe, he liked to think, from a time before she was with Doug. Is that why she was looking so kind and happy, instead of always so fierce?

'Nick, it's you to bet,' said Simon. Of course, the slower people were at betting, the longer for him to take their money.

'Sorry. OK, call the eight,' said Nick.

Alan dealt the fourth card, and Nick turned back to the table. It was the queen of diamonds. So, the hearts flush was gone, but the straight was very much a possibility, and a good one too – hard to imagine Simon could possibly have it beaten. But of course if he didn't have the straight then he had nothing, and what's more, Simon would know that.

'Twenty pounds,' said Simon.

Nick looked at him sadly. Simon had seen the danger and was going to drive him out. Well, fuck him. Simon could take the fucking pot. He'd been in this situation too many times before. For once, he was going to do the sensible thing, minimise his losses and feel good about it afterwards.

'Fold,' said Nick.

Although he was now far from sure if that had been the right thing to do or not. That was the problem with folding – it always left things so unresolved. Had he lost his nerve and walked away from a big win? Had he really been smart or just wilfully stupid? When it came to making decisions, big or small, major career choices or bets at poker, his record was hardly impressive.

Not knowing anyone in Oxford, and not wanted at home, Nick had had to go somewhere. Perhaps unwisely for a young man with no money, university degree or friends, Nick moved to London in the middle of a recession. It was the 1980s – London was a post-industrial but pre-ironic demolition site, and he had to struggle through a humourless decade of mass unemployment and bad pop music. Too nervous to squat or go on the dole and no appetite, connections or skills for the black market, he had moved into a bedsit and worked in a furniture-distribution centre on the edge of North London. It was itinerant, badly paid temporary work that he did for six years.

He stayed in London for the duration of an entire economic cycle. To begin with, he was poor and scruffy and a bit desperate, and so was everyone and everything else. By the end, he was still poor, but everyone else had got richer. In truth, he had never really felt at home in that uncomfortable and exhausting city, but it was now changing in ways he hadn't ever expected or wanted. Working-class culture, the only culture that had ever even tried to accommodate him, was disintegrating. Like the red squirrel, it wasn't so much being defeated as moved on, displaced. People were giving up smoking, snooker halls were closing down and the pinball machines were being taken out of the pubs. For a while he had got into the habit of going to football matches, but he stopped as they became less an outlet for tribal hatreds, and more a moderately expensive form of entertainment. He was no longer the cleverest and most interesting person who worked at the warehouse – there was now someone there who had *finished* his degree at Oxford, who would talk about Nietzsche and do cryptic crosswords in the tea break.

He moved from bedsit to bedsit, each one further and further out but just as expensive, and he didn't share them with Irish builders or Welsh carpenters any more, but with Bosnians and Nigerians. He still owned almost nothing, but irritatingly he kept getting robbed, probably by his neighbours – on top of everything else, he was becoming a bit racist. And, after all that, it turned out that he did need an education. Not at Oxford, and anyway they weren't about to have him back, but he needed to go somewhere. That was obvious. It was now the 1990s. Even stupid people went to university, and if you didn't go, you had to be talented at something like football or music or business, or else rich or really lucky. Otherwise you were fucked.

It was better this time. At Oxford he had been much like everyone else, except less posh or good at writing essays. This time round, at Reading, studying English literature on a thirty-year-old campus instead of at a four-hundred-year-old college, he was a much more exotic proposition. He was older than his classmates and, although never particularly well built, his arms and wrists were thicker than the eighteen-year-old boys' he sat next to, his voice richer and his face more textured. He could talk knowledgeably about things that no one else knew anything about. For a twenty-seven-year-old, his stock of stories wasn't perhaps as dramatic as it should have been – travelling on London night buses, pilfering stock from warehouses, drinking and swearing with bricklayers, watching bands play in empty pubs before they became semi-famous, the occasional industrial accident, but it was enough to impress his new peer group. What's more, if never an outstanding academic success, he was at least above average at his studies. It helped that the students were lazier and shyer than last time, and the tutors kinder. But more importantly, at some point over the years, he had *matured*, a little: he could speak in tutorials without blushing and write confident essays about post-structuralism. He even liked reading books now.

Having taken so long to get to university this second time, Nick was in no hurry to get back out again. If his experience of living in a modern economy had taught him one thing, it was that he wasn't well suited to it. But once again his timing was off. It was now the late 1990s, he was over thirty and the government wasn't about to give him any more money, not unless he was going to study something really practical or really hard. When it came to it, there wasn't any choice, and perhaps that was for the best. He had already made all the important choices in his life, and look where that had got him. This time round, there would be no funny business – he was going to do exactly what was expected of him. With neither hope nor desperation, and only a little sadness, he applied to be a teacher.

It was now almost midnight. Doug didn't like games to go on any later. The only people who ever did were Simon, who wanted the chance to win more money, and Nick, who wanted the chance to win his money back. Alan dealt the cards for the last time, giving Nick the two and eight of clubs – well, there might be something on here.

'Bet three pounds,' said Simon.

'Call three,' said Vijay.

'I'm happy to play with you boys for that,' said Doug.

'Call,' said Nick.

'Fold,' said Alan.

Down came the flop. The five of clubs, the king of spades and the jack of hearts. That meant Nick had three clubs altogether, a chance of a flush, with nothing else on. Was that enough to keep going? It was generally at this point, he knew, that he ought to start concentrating.

'Five pounds,' said Simon.

'Call,' said Vijay.

'In my opinion that sounds like a very reasonable bet,' said Doug, in his signature camp, hugely irritating Sean Connery voice. It could normally be expected at least once a night and, Nick knew, was invariably a bad sign – it meant he was almost certainly sitting on something good.

'Call,' said Nick.

Alan dealt the fourth card on to the table – the six of spades. So that had been a waste of five pounds. Still, at least this wasn't going to cost him any more money. Even if it was the last hand of the night, he was happy to be watching rather than playing this one. Nick could see that, this time round, Simon wasn't being so eager, and he didn't look too happy about Vijay still being in.

After a short but still noticeable pause, he said, 'Five pounds.'

Now it was Vijay's turn to do some thinking. This could take a while. If he was to add it up, how many hours had Nick spent waiting for Vijay to make a bet? He was a fucking human calculating machine. A really slow one, who ponderously worked out the statistical probability of holding the winning hand, and then laboriously calibrated it against the size of the pot. Well, whatever else, at least Nick didn't play his poker like *that*. Finally, just as Simon was about to say something, Vijay called the bet.

'I'm more than happy with that,' said Doug immediately, throwing in his chips with exaggerated nonchalance.

'Fold,' said Nick.

Simon badly wanted to win from Doug, that was obvious. Christ knows why – you'd have thought he'd made enough money tonight. And how much did Doug want to win from Simon? Not as much – he was at home, he was already comfortably up and in good spirits. He wasn't desperate to win this hand – he was staying in simply because he thought that he would. Nick was sure of it.

One of the things that Nick had noticed over the years was that he was a pretty good poker player – provided, that is, he wasn't actually *playing*. He could coolly analyse the others' ambitions and moods. He could guess what they were holding with confidence and precision and even some accuracy. The betting was no longer a semiotic maelstrom, a bewildering jumble of missed signals, mistakes and ambiguities, but instead a reasoned exchange of information. He would sit, calmly and good-humouredly, watching them play, smiling quietly to himself as it unfolded exactly as he had expected. So why the fuck couldn't he do it when it mattered?

Was it performance anxiety? Did he lack the nerve to stay grounded, and make quick, sensible decisions? It was almost certainly a class thing, and maybe even a race thing too – Vijay had that Indian sensibility, where he could inscrutably and irritatingly smile away when all kinds of shit was going on. Doug wasn't posh, of course, but it turned out that he had gone to a public school, albeit one of those backward Scottish ones where all they do is beat the hell out of each other, and all you get taught is rugby and chemistry and how to sound like you're English. Still, even that had been enough to instil in him some sort of officer-class mentality: to hold your nerve, show leadership when most needed and be *good in a crisis*. Well, Nick was shit in a crisis.

So, the last card – the ten of spades. Nick was watching them closely, more closely than he ever managed to do when he was playing. He thought he could see a tremor of excitement on Vijay's face before it resumed its normal plump and contented state. That card had clearly been good news. But Doug meanwhile was incapable of hiding his delight. His face was theatrically reconfiguring itself every two or three seconds, his eyes beaming and then frowning with exaggerated grumpiness, his mouth puckering and then tightening. Simon, of course, looked exactly the same as ever.

'Check,' said Simon, who knew the game was up.

Vijay was hungrily eyeing up the pot. There was none of his careful probability and risk assessment this time. He was just counting up how much money was in the middle of the table, and how much he had in front of him.

'Bet twenty-five pounds,' said Vijay.

But Doug wasn't waiting around either. 'Meet your twenty-five, and I'll raise another thirty,' he said.

'Fold,' said Simon.

Nick could see that neither of them was bluffing. They both had spade flushes, but one of them would have to have the better one. This was going to be messy. Simon, who was obviously irritated that he'd stayed in for as long as he had, was scowling while Alan could hardly bear to look. Oh Christ, thought Nick, *don't let Doug win this*.

This time Vijay paused. He was clearly well aware of the situation – whoever had the highest spade would win this. It didn't look as if Vijay was holding the ace, but was Doug? Hard to say. Nick could see that Vijay's options were limited. He could raise again if he really wanted, but Doug was going to stick it out whatever. And he could hardly fold, not now. The pot was worth a hundred and fifty pounds. Vijay's soft face was apprehensive, maybe even a bit sorrowful. He was taking his time, but he wasn't calculating – he was preparing himself for what was about to happen next.

'OK, I'll call thirty pounds,' he said.

They both flicked over their cards. No wonder Vijay had been betting so forcefully. He had the jack and the five of spades – that made a flush with the king on the table as the highest card, followed by his jack. Not that that mattered much, because Doug had the queen and three of spades – a flush with the king followed by the queen. Doug, that insufferable fucker, by the very narrowest of margins, had done it.

Nick gulped. This had been easily the hand of the night, probably the biggest hand for months, and thank God he hadn't been involved. Alan was clearly thinking much the same thing and seemed more frazzled than ever, and even Simon was looking a bit startled. Meanwhile, Vijay looked like he might start crying at any moment. There was a chorus of sympathetic wails.

It was a *hospital hand*, said Doug, by now hopelessly over-excited and not making Vijay feel any better at all. The kind of hand, Doug went on needlessly to explain, that, if played well, would lead to certain disaster. Simon assured Vijay that he would have played it exactly the same way, Alan was help-fully trying to estimate the extraordinary improbability of such a thing happening, but by now Vijay was inconsolable. He had lost nearly a hundred pounds on the turn of a card. Poor greedy little Vijay. And lucky, lucky Doug.

Nick didn't believe in God. Not even as a kid – he'd always instinctively known it was bound to be a con. Nor was he in the least bit superstitious. As someone who had laboured to become a member of the educated middle class, he knew it was important to despise star signs, astrology and other such deviations from the Enlightenment project, and he always made a point of making irrevocable judgements on those colleagues who read their horoscopes in the staff room – who were, he noticed, and also noticed that he noticed, invariably female or gay. He was also impressively resistant to omens: black cats, broken mirrors, mascots, gypsy curses and all the other hocus-pocus that second-rate people used to navigate their lives. He had even taken the opportunity to marry Janet on Friday the 13th, as a daring and, he had thought, slightly amusing declaration of his contempt for superstition, though he sometimes regretted this now.

All of this was if not paradoxical then at least surprising, because one of the very few things he did believe in was luck. It was a powerful and cosmic force, something omniscient and fundamental that permeated and shaped the universe and everything in it – like gravity or background radiation. What was luck? What was it made of? Nick had surprisingly few metaphysical concerns about it. Unlike everything else, Nick had never applied his usual jeering scepticism to luck. Luck was just luck, and he had accepted it with no more than a nod and a shrug. Of course, there were plenty of things that could either make you or ruin you, like class or cancer or race or shit genes or rich parents or the latitude and era you were born in – Nick knew all about these, in fact had spent much of his life getting worried and cross about them. But these weren't alternatives to luck, they were just its manifestations. And if he stopped believing in luck, well then, what was he going to do? He was hardly about to become a fucking *Marxist*.

Where was it? Well, obviously you couldn't see luck – but you could see its effects all right. You only had to look at the world, with its winners and losers, its lopsided distribution of wealth and happiness, its vicious circles and positive-feedback loops, its tragic allocation of gifts and forfeits. You could see it at school, in the boys with their hard little faces, shiny hair and presumptuous smiles, and the others – the ones with the sad eyes and shuffling feet. You could see it in Reading bus station on a wet Saturday afternoon. No, you didn't have to go far to see what luck was. You only had to look at what went on round the poker table. In fact, you only had to look at Doug.

In his office at home, which he'd recently experimented with referring to as his study, Doug had four quotations, each painted in black italics on a lacquered wooden block. It had been one of Sophia's ideas, which was not necessarily a guarantee of total brilliance, but he had been pleased to find out that many of history's great generals had done something similar. And he had to acknowledge the study had needed something. It was only comparatively recently that he had learnt that having a big house with large rooms and high ceilings wasn't enough – you had to fill them with good stuff. Flat-screen televisions and state-of-the-art stereos didn't cut it any more, though they still had those, of course. You had to have *really* good stuff. Old things, pretty things, unusual things, things that could generate rich conversation. All the kind of stuff that Sophia knew about. At least this idea had been cheaper than her others, and he had even been allowed to choose the quotes himself.

He had nailed the first one above his door, in direct line of sight whenever he looked up from his desk. It was a favourite saying from one of his favourite sporting heroes, the golfer

Arnold Palmer: *The more I practise, the luckier I get.* The force of it, the sheer North American hard-headed good sense of it never failed to stir him. Arnold Palmer – winner of the Masters no fewer than four times, global pioneer of the casual sportswear industry, and why? Simple: because he practised, that's why.

On his desk itself, a jet-black modern affair, designed to accommodate not pens or paper clips or pads of paper, but his desktop computer, laser-jet printer, phone charger and electronic organiser, was another block. This one was his old school motto, *Ex opus opes*. Wealth comes from work. Doug knew this to be true. Everything he had ever done and seen in his life confirmed it. He only had to look at his brother, at his schoolfriends, at his business competitors, at his father-in-law and at his fellow poker players to know this.

Doug was wealthy. That was indisputable. And the source of his wealth had nothing to do with his physical strength, as impressive as that had once been, nor his education come to that. It didn't even have much to do with talent. His brother had been born with all the talent in the family, and look where that had got him. And it had nothing, absolutely nothing, to do with luck. Luck, Doug had always known, was for losers. Nobody who talked about luck ever won anything – not in the end. Sure, anyone could win the odd hand now and again, but the poker players who worried about luck were the ones who lost money to the ones who never did. Luck was just an excuse, a lie. An excuse for not practising like Arnold Palmer, for not being determined and single-minded like him, and for not working hard enough.

The third block was on the wall facing the door, behind his chair and above his library of marketing textbooks, executive memoirs, sporting biographies and nearly a dozen guides to playing better poker. This one was something that Sophia had once quoted to him: *The philosophers have only interpreted the world . . . the point is to change it.* Even if Simon was unlikely ever to see it, Doug just *had* to have it up on his wall. Doug wasn't like Simon, or Nick for that matter. He didn't moan or teach or philosophise. Doug did things. That was why he was an entrepreneur, a deal-maker, a doer. It was why, with the most rudimentary of business plans, he had set up the gym in a basement on Wycombe Street all those years ago.

Back then a private gymnasium was unheard of in Reading. Everyone assumed it was just a front for a brothel. Of course, that was partly because it *had* been – at least in its first incarnation. It was owned by Doug's cousin who, in his naivety, had assumed that the only way to make money was to do something that was against the law and so had set up a half-hearted little massage-and-tanning centre, which was entirely cross-subsidised by prostitution. But back in those days, it had been an extremely challenging sector to be in. It was before European immigration had made the labour market flexible, the customer base was static and impoverished and they were frequently getting raided by the small-minded local police force. Doug's cousin abandoned it, leaving him in charge with instructions to wind the business down and sell up. Instead, Doug borrowed ten thousand pounds and decided to go legitimate.

The move paid off almost immediately. It was 1992 and Reading was entering the longest economic boom in its history. The town was filling up with new kinds of people: telecommunications engineers, database programmers, biotechnology researchers, graphic designers, intellectual-property lawyers, management consultants and organisational psychologists. It seemed they had little interest in prostitutes, but they loved going to the gym all the time – provided it wasn't run by the council or accessible to the rest of the general public.

Doug could sense things. Just like all his business heroes, he didn't bother with economic forecasts or market surveys, but relied instead on his instincts – his natural ability to sense the mood in the Irish-theme bars, under the atrium of shopping centres and in the ready-meals aisle of supermarkets. The 1990s, he knew, was his decade. He had been too young for the 1980s and anyway, as far as he could tell, he hadn't missed all that much. It seemed to him that the only people who made money in the 1980s were either really clever, like the ones who knew about computers, or else rich already, like stockbrokers. Doug wasn't either of those things. He was never going to be a yuppie – he came from *Fife*, for a start. And the others, the ones who weren't getting rich – the miners and ship builders and steel makers and farmers and the Welsh and Scottish, well, they all just got fucked.

But this decade was different. In the 1990s, any stupid wanker could make money. People who designed T-shirts or owned nightclubs or had a website or made organic fruit juice or imported vintage sports cars or sold advertising space on the back of bus tickets – they were all raking it in. You didn't need to be posh, though it probably still helped, and you didn't even need to know about anything. In fact, all you really had to do was buy something, a house preferably, but it could be pretty much anything, and then sell it again a bit later. But, as it was, Doug did know about something. He knew about sports, physical exercise, training programmes and health and fitness. More importantly, he knew about the people who did these things. He understood the kind of seriousness they brought to recreation: their sombre pursuit of physical well-being, their continual need to set and exceed targets, and their dislike of amateurism or anything that suggested that what they were doing wasn't necessary and important.

Very soon the little basement on Wycombe Street was at capacity. Doug's machines, bought as a job lot from a closed-down municipal leisure complex, were the most modern in Berkshire. In what proved to be a significant market innovation, he kept it open eighteen hours a day to cater for the early-morning and late-night professional class who were not prepared to compromise their commitment to either work or personal fitness, and he stocked a quasi-legal range of muscle-tissue-enhancement products. He rehired all of the girls from the brothel days, who made for very popular receptionists and fitness instructors. He went round the major employers at the business park and negotiated corporate membership deals. None of this was especially difficult – it wasn't *philosophy* or anything, but he was good at it.

By 1997, Doug owned four executive health clubs (no one called them gyms any more): two in Reading, and others in High Wycombe and Swindon. To all intents and purposes he was a millionaire, but the intuitive connection to his customers was as strong as ever. The muscle powders and potions had gone and instead his clubs now had the exclusive UK licence to sell a range of high-end sportswear designed for the Canadian 1996 Olympic Team. Once a week they held women-only sessions, and he had hired, at incredible expense, a bespoke consultancy from London to come up with an integrated-brand concept for the clubs' interiors, façades and all of his communications materials. Doug still knew what was going on all right – he had even voted Labour in the general election.

It was around this time that he embarked on his most important series of negotiations. Doug had a rival – Andreas Lakis. Older and more established, Lakis had moved out of tanning salons and massage parlours as early as the 1980s, and owned seven clubs across the South of England. But Lakis wasn't like Doug. He was too cautious, and was disengaged from his customers. His centres were poorly ventilated and badly lit – they looked like they were run by local authorities, and the girls who worked there weren't very pretty. Lakis competed on price, of all things, and as a result they were used by working-class males and nobody else. They were still making money of course, everyone was making money, but nowhere near enough. And as Doug well knew, it wasn't about making money any more – it was about making *real* money.

Doug made him an audacious and insulting offer. An offer so undermining and aggressive that Lakis refused outright to even consider selling his clubs, and instead suggested that they merge the two businesses. He well knew that he was old and out of touch, he knew that his clubs needed new investment and ideas. There was something else as well – Lakis had a daughter. Not as young as Doug would have wanted, but ideal in lots of other ways. She was handsome with striking black hair and dark-red lips, and she had the kind of fine Southern European figure that Doug knew would last. She was as smart and hard-headed as her father, but better educated. She had been a teacher, just like Nick, but unlike Nick she had actually wanted to be one – at least for a while, before she got bored and went to work for the family business instead.

Crucially, Sophia Lakis herself seemed willing to sleep with Doug and maybe even to fall in love with him. This was particularly important because frustratingly no one else would. He was thirty-five years old, he was successful, he drove a car that was big and expensive. He felt in great mental and physical shape and women *still* didn't want to have sex with him. This, it seemed, was one of the downsides of the 1990s – being wealthy wasn't enough these days, it didn't count the way it used to, now that so many half-wits were rich as well. No, you had to actually look good, either that or be famous, and Doug was never going to be either of those things.

Although he wouldn't have ever described himself as ugly, Doug knew that he was, at the very least, the opposite of good-looking. He had a rugby player's physique, which was fine as far as it went, but he also had a rugby player's face – crudely put together, with small, deep-set eyes, the inevitable broken nose and meaty lips. His neck was too short and he had to dress carefully, for without a suit he looked like a low-profile member of the semi-criminal classes – a bouncer or bodyguard or debt collector. If it had been another era he might have had a kind of honest, hard-working, battered appeal, but by the end of the twentieth century nobody went for that any more. None of the men at his centres wanted to look like that – they all wanted well-defined stomachs and to look pretty. In fact, what they really all wanted was to look like girls.

Within twelve months of meeting, Sophia and Doug got married in Cyprus. By this time Doug was Managing Director of Lakis-McLain Enterprises Ltd, and his father-in-law was Chairman. Sophia's hopelessly unreliable brother was the Marketing Director but that was fair enough because Doug's idiot cousin had turned up again and was Sales Director, and anyway neither of them was allowed to make any decisions. Lakis liked it that way, and so did Doug. They had quickly discovered how much they had in common – a vigorous work ethic, a suspicion of all governments and political parties, a strong appreciation for the importance of the family and a passionate determination to pay as little tax as possible. They were both Christians as well, without being too bothered that they were different types.

Even before they were married, Sophia was pregnant with the twins, and three months before Alexis and Olympia were born, they had already profitably consolidated their respective properties and bought the biggest house on Kingsbury

Road in the heart of Caversham, the best neighbourhood in Reading. It took another year before the house was refurbished, but that was fine – that was exactly the kind of thing that Sophia liked doing and she had overseen the whole process. It couldn't have been easier – he had achieved in just a couple of years what everyone else spent their entire twenties and thirties striving for, and all he'd had to do was read a few contracts and write some cheques.

Doug's last block was smaller and kept securely locked in his top-right desk drawer, nestling on top of his collection of pornographic magazines, which he had gradually accumulated over the years and knew was problematic, but had somehow never found quite the right moment to get rid of. This block was different from the others. Sophia had chosen it, and had even written it out herself – first in Greek, and then below translated into English. Unfortunately, given his dislike of philosophers, this was a quote from an ancient Greek philosopher. It said: *Call no man happy before he dies, he is at best but fortunate.* Doug wasn't sure if he liked it. It didn't really fit with the others, it wasn't the kind of thing he could ever imagine Arnold Palmer saying, and he wasn't sure what Sophia was getting at: did she just mean that they shouldn't take what they had for granted? Well, he was all for that, or did it mean that she was unhappy? Or did she think he was unhappy? Was he, in some sort of deep and important way that he hadn't fathomed yet?

Once, when he was hungover and melancholic and tired and bored, he had absent-mindedly opened the drawer and seen the block for the first time in months. He wasn't sure why, but it had made him cry, a little.

Round at Nick's – March

'Three pounds,' said Nick.

'Call,' said Simon.

'Call,' said Vijay.

'Call,' said Alan.

'Not a chance,' said Doug.

Doug turned the fourth card up on to the table. Well, well – the eight of spades. Already showing were the eight of diamonds, the jack of hearts and the nine of spades. In his hand, Vijay had the eight and four of clubs. So he had three eights – at this stage, at any stage, that was very good indeed. Not, of course, one of the *great* hands, and there was always a chance, about twelve per cent, that one of them had the other eight.

'Five pounds,' said Nick.

'Fold,' said Simon.

So clearly Simon didn't have the eight. But what about Nick? It had to be considered. Or perhaps he was trying to make something else? There were two spades showing on the table, so if Nick had two more spades in his hand then he could be on for the flush. Or else, and this was probably more likely, he was going for the straight. Either of those and Vijay's three eights wouldn't count for anything.

'Call the five,' said Vijay, 'and raise another five.'

'Fold,' said Alan.

'Call,' said Nick.

So it was just the two of them. He'd knocked out Alan with his raise, but Nick had stayed with him. That was fine, he shouldn't be worried yet – after all if he had the best hand, then he wanted someone, particularly Nick, to stay in with him. But then Doug dealt the final card, and that changed absolutely everything. It could hardly have been worse – the ten of spades! No wonder Doug greeted it with a loud and exaggerated intake of breath. It meant, of course, that the flush was still feasible, but more alarmingly, with the eight, nine, ten and jack all now showing on the table a straight was looking more than just a possibility.

Vijay gave a little shudder as he frantically began his next set of calculations, but he knew it wasn't so much trepidation as excitement. Either that or it could be the cold – Nick's house was never warm enough. At least Simon's, for all its other problems, tended to be well heated. Better than Doug's, which actually wasn't much better than Nick's, though he did have the excuse that his house was so much bigger. Vijay himself spent a great deal of money on heating, on ensuring that his house was as warm as possible for family and guests. It was, surely, a basic responsibility of the head of any household, and now that he had designated the spare bedroom as an office, it was even tax-deductible. So why wasn't Nick able to manage it? Yes, he always gave them lots of wine and beer to drink, but he must know there was more to hosting a game of cards than that?

Well, never mind that for now – he needed to concentrate, he needed to work out whether Nick had a better hand than him. The chance of Nick having the two spades for a flush wasn't so very high – about five per cent. But the chance of him having a queen or a seven to make the straight was almost exactly thirty-three per cent. Then, of course, there was still the possibility that he had the other eight. And if he had the other eight, what else did he have? Vijay's other card was just a four, but Nick could easily have a high card, higher than anything else showing. And what about the full house? Ideally, of course, he should work all of this out. But he needed so much more time.

'I bet twenty pounds,' said Nick.

Vijay peered carefully across at him, but there were no clues there. Reading faces wasn't what Vijay was good at, and besides – it was difficult to even *see* Nick's face. It was too dark, one of the lights in the room didn't seem to be working, and Nick was at the far end of the enormous table. Vijay still wasn't sure what to make of Nick's poker table. It was undeniably impressive, it was certainly something that he would like to have in his own house, but for some reason, despite poker being its sole purpose, it wasn't very easy to play on.

Vijay turned to the pot and started counting. This, after all, was the real issue. Everything depended on how much was in there. Ultimately, the probabilities of the cards and the size of Nick's bet were meaningless unless one also knew the returns. And in this case they were considerable, more than one would have thought. There was very nearly eighty pounds sitting in the middle of the table, and he needed to pay just twenty pounds for a chance of taking it all. So this is what it came down to: the odds were four to one, and he had an approximately fifty per cent chance of winning.

Of course, if Nick had bet forty or fifty pounds, then that would have been a different matter. That would have been a more difficult bet to call – so difficult, in fact, that he would most probably have folded. So why hadn't he? Was it because Nick *wanted* Vijay to bet – that he was certain of victory, but

45

wanted to take another twenty pounds from him? Yes, quite possibly – in which case he needed to think twice about this. But there again, if Nick was so sure of his cards, wouldn't he have done better to have made a much larger bet – isn't that what he himself would have done? Or maybe he didn't have the cards at all, and thought that a big bet would be too obvious a bluff. Was Nick playing a cleverer game than Vijay? Or was he just being too clever?

Nick was tapping a chip on the table, trying to hurry him along, trying to push him into a decision – but which one? Did he want to scare him off, or bring him on? As for the others, there were the usual signs of impatience and bad manners. There was a shifting in their seats. Doug was snorting, and complaining that he was getting cramp behind the table, and Simon was twitching his head and clicking his tongue irritably. No one said anything, no one normally did, but they all wanted him to get on with it as quickly as possible, which meant that they all wanted him to stop thinking.

Vijay was not a man of strong views. True, he had voted Conservative in every general election, he thought that taxes were too high and that people who worked for the government were lazy. And he was happy enough to believe in a god, just as long as it didn't mean that he had to actually do anything about it or give away any money. But none of these were things that he cared too much about. No, the one and only thing he firmly did believe in was unhurried and reasoned decision-making, taken in as much time as was required. It was, after all, the basis for sound accountancy, and it was the failure to adhere to this principle that explained why practically the whole world had got itself into such a mess. Just look at what was going on! Investment bankers, property speculators, revolutionary terrorists … none of them bothered to take enough time. None of them ever paused long enough to think things through, to carefully consider all of the relevant factors and possible consequences. It also explained why Nick was so bad at poker.

'OK,' he said at last. 'I'll see you for twenty pounds.'

Vijay could see Nick grimace. Whatever his bet might have been trying to suggest, he clearly hadn't wanted Vijay to call him. There was no straight or flush there. But did he have the other eight? No, he was shaking his head, and Vijay was sure now – he didn't have that either.

'I think you've got me beat – I've got a pair of tens.'

Vijay showed his three eights and Nick nodded silently. Vijay could see what had happened – Nick *had* been trying for the straight, and with a ten in his hand he had stood a reasonable chance until the last card had come up, giving him the pair but nothing more. Feeling generous, he could see that there had been some logic there, even if Nick hadn't played very well. And now he felt the familiar glow of rich satisfaction, as with both hands he scooped the pot towards him across the table, and it gently collided with his own well-ordered stack of chips.

It was hard to calculate how much he loved poker night. He loved winning of course, and he loved counting his winnings, just as he liked counting everyone else's scores, and opening fresh packs of cards, and meticulously shuffling the deck, and solemnly exchanging bank-notes for multicoloured chips at the beginning and end of each evening. But the thing that he liked best about it was *playing* poker. He had fallen in love with the game immediately, as soon as he'd grasped its computational challenges and infinite chains of reasoning. Of course, he had always liked board games and logic puzzles, but poker was both easier and so much more difficult – besides, he was an accountant and, with no money involved, other games always ran the risk of being fundamentally pointless. But no one, *no one*, could ever describe poker as pointless.

Who cared if the others sometimes behaved badly or drank too much? OK, it would be nice if they could be a bit more patient, but all he really wanted was for them to take the game as seriously as he did, to play their poker in a determined and thoughtful manner. And you would never accuse Simon and Doug, not to mention Nick, of not being determined enough. No, when he considered it, he couldn't think of a single more enjoyable way to spend his time and, on a night like this, playing with scientific rigour and winning so deservedly, he didn't even mind having to be at Nick's house.

Home advantage – one of the most primitive and universal rules of nature. Nick had read the literature. It was a scientific fact. It was a *sociological* fact. Two-thirds of all contests are won by the home side. Across all sports, across all competitions, across all species, the same rule held. It applied to football teams, basketball players, boxers, sticklebacks, fighting dogs, roosters and earwigs. So why the fuck didn't it apply to him? Why was it that, every time, *every time*, they came to his house, he was the one who got fucked?

It didn't help of course that he had, if not the smallest house, then certainly the most shit. That was incontrovertible – he'd spent an evening researching house prices on the internet. He lived on the least desirable road in a neighbourhood with the worst schools, highest crime rate and poorest people. OK, it was Reading rather than Calcutta, and the houses had all been built from brick in the 1930s rather than concrete in the 1960s, but the one opposite had had a mattress in its front garden for more than a year now and, as far as he could tell, everyone on Milton Road who wasn't on social security was a teacher.

At the end of the road there was a clump of shops, which had been optimistically named Milton Parade. It was a dispiriting sight. There were two little groceries side by side which bafflingly sold exactly the same limited range of products at the same prices, and were both run by middle-aged South Asian men who Nick was incapable of telling apart. Aside from that, there was a launderette, a *launderette* for Christ's sake, a shamelessly disgusting Chinese takeaway, and a former bookmaker's, which after going bankrupt had been vacant for two years during which time Nick had gently nurtured hopes of a delicatessen or bookshop or one of those independent, naively managed cafés that stocked exclusively the liberal daily broadsheets, had excellent home-made carrot cake and pretty young waitresses who came over without asking to refill your cup with fresh coffee. But in the end it had been let to another bookmaker.

So his house was not going to intimidate them. In fact, nowadays, the only person it intimidated was himself. It was difficult to tell whether it was the house or Nick who most disliked the other. If he was alone on a wet Sunday afternoon he felt cornered, trapped by it. The walls, not painted now for ten years, as Janet had given up reminding him, were menacing and oppressive, the dark-cream finish having gradually congealed into a greasy yellow. The ill-fitting window frames rattled excitedly in the wind, the floorboards creaked unnaturally and the walls shuddered whenever the small suburban bus rolled past. Of course, it wasn't grand enough to be haunted, but Nick was convinced that a previous occupant had done something despicable and violent to someone else in there.

And then there were the paintings. The paintings had all been bought seven years ago, when Nick had decided, for reasons he was no longer certain about, to use what little money he had to cultivate a collection of contemporary art. And Janet, not knowing anything about art other than to be suspicious, but also a little bit impressed, had reluctantly gone along with it.

These had been hopeful times. It was the new century and he, in some important ways, was also new. He was recently married, and owned a house. He had a job, a proper grown-up job, which he didn't yet hate, and they even, largely thanks to Janet, had a small amount of savings. He was returning to London (in a car!) and, if not in triumph, then at least with a purpose. He was going to buy some art. He had announced it to everyone he knew, brought it up in conversation whenever he met someone for the first time, and generally made it the cornerstone of his personality. He subscribed to specialist magazines and mailing lists, pretended that he wasn't a teacher and cheerfully lied about how much money he was looking to spend, and very soon he was getting invited to private views and gallery receptions. Even Janet had enjoyed those, having soon realised that Nick wasn't the kind of husband to take his wife to a restaurant, the theatre or anywhere really. These trips were an opportunity to spend money on pretty clothes and be charmed by young men with long eyelashes who wanted to sell them things.

But he had chosen poorly. He had never really understood much about visual art, except that he must in no circumstances be led by his own uninformed petit-bourgeois notions of artistic conformity, and certainly not by Janet's insistence that they look nice. Instead, he had selected art works on the basis of their striking distinctiveness, their originality, their radical subversion of traditional aesthetic norms and their capacity to disturb and provoke the viewer into new states of awareness and political engagement.

The consequences of this were still all around him. Not only were the paintings worthless, they also looked horrible. A series of macabre portraits, lurid landscapes and hyperviolent group compositions, all characterised by their extensive use of primary colours, discordant imagery, jarring perspectives and brutal symbolism. They looked, as Janet's bloody annoying sixteen-year-old cousin once observed, *mental*. Although interestingly, after years of living with them, Nick had come to the conclusion that just about the only thing they *didn't* look was original, strikingly distinctive or especially radical.

If they had been painted by Picasso in the 1920s then he supposed they would have been masterpieces. If they had been done by pretty much any European Jew or Gypsy in the 1930s then they could have been heroic fractured responses to totalitarianism. And if they had been done in the 1960s by one of Andy Warhol's fuck-head mates who had then abruptly gone and died in a controversial drugs stunt, then they could have been devastating and prophetic critiques of American consumer capitalism. But no. These had all been done by a group of well-fed young artists in London at the beginning of the twenty-first century, none of whom had been particularly alienated or gone on to do anything else of any importance, and all of whom, as far as he knew, were still alive. As a result the pictures were valueless and largely without any artistic merit. Well, it had been an expensive process, but at least now he understood about art.

The furniture, too, had been a mistake, inherited from his father, who had in turn inherited it from his. He had been taken by the idea of being surrounded by family heirlooms. Not antiques or anything, but *old stuff*. Like almost everything else that had fucked him up, it was largely a class thing. He had somehow got it into his head that being surrounded by old things would give him a sense of authority and maybe even wisdom, that whatever one might say about his house or job or street or wife, at least he wasn't the kind of man who had to buy new furniture. And, as a result, his house had for some years now resembled one of those dingy junk shops on the Oxford Road.

Nick had no sense of what period or style or wood the furniture was. Once one evening, when some of his adult education students had come round to drink beer with him, someone had asked him what his bookcases were made from and, not knowing any better but also knowing that neither would they, he'd announced that it was *dark wood*. For all he could say with any confidence was that his furniture was very dark, almost black, and that it absorbed what little light the mean windows and murky walls allowed. But whether they had always been that colour or had just got darker over the years with dirt and dust and sadness he didn't know.

It was all this, of course, which had led to the biggest mistake of them all – the great card-table folly. Desperate for some kind of advantage, some hints or deep strategy or fuck knows, some way of cheating, he had been trawling through the internet late at night, as with most nights, when he came across a specialist American supplier of poker furniture and accessories. Buried on its website was a one-off sale of a discontinued line of professional poker tables.

The ProPokerPlus! was a thing of extraordinary beauty. Even the small low-resolution photographs made that abundantly clear. Marvellously proportioned, with gracefully curved but sturdy teak legs, it had a dark-green baize top and ash-wood border that shimmered under the lights of a casino. The whole thing radiated all the things he didn't have – power, confidence, nobility and affluence. And so, with amazing recklessness, he had gone and bought it then and there. It was the only major item of furniture he had ever chosen and paid for himself. It was incredibly expensive – in total, it cost more than the sum of all his losses at cards and, despite lying significantly about its price, it had provoked a savage and long-running row with Janet.

It was one of the stupidest things he'd ever done. He'd realised that almost immediately, and several times had been on the point of cancelling the order, but, anxious about his own fearfulness, not to mention the deposit, he had manfully, idiotically gone through with it. But the moronic horror of what he'd done didn't become apparent until the thing arrived six weeks later. It looked shit, it looked ridiculous. So inappropriate and ungainly in his living room that that fucker Doug had offered to do him a favour and buy it from him. The problem was not the table itself. For once, Nick hadn't been let down by capitalism – it was as impressive and beautiful as the website promised it would be. No wonder Doug had wanted it for his place. No, that wasn't the problem. The problem, of course, was that his house was too fucking small.

He had toyed with the idea of buying a bigger house, or at least getting an extension built. But even the briefest of investigations had made it apparent that this wasn't an option. That really would have been madness and, in all probability, divorce. For the melancholy and mundane truth was that he didn't have enough money. He was a teacher for fuck's sake – they never had enough money. Nor was there any prospect of getting some from anywhere else. His parents were, thank God, both dead and the tiny, begrudging inheritance long gone. Once upon a time, he had had hopes of Janet, who was an only child, the product of elderly parents from marginally more prosperous stock, but instead he had had to endure his mother-in-law's robust physical health and total mental collapse – a lethal combination, which had meant for years now she had sat senseless and happy in a private care home costing £700 per week. Nor was Janet ever going to bring in much money herself – she worked in Social Services, doing some kind of management or administrative or policy role, which he really ought to know more about. All he knew for sure was that she took it very seriously, had a number of work friends who were difficult to tell apart, and that she earned even less than him. No, it was no good nurturing fantasies about a new house. He would in all likelihood die in this house, or else something smaller. Other than winning the Lottery, which he despised and also secretly entered every single week, there was no way out.

And, of course, the table had made no difference at all: he still lost at home. If anything, and Vijay's spreadsheets certainly seemed to say so, he now lost more than ever. The ProPokerPlus! didn't embolden or encourage him – it mocked him. It made him look stupid. Like the decrepit furniture, like the paintings on the walls, like the walls themselves, like the whole fucking house, like the mattress in the neighbour's garden and the useless corner shops, it howled with one voice the same deadly message: that Nick was a loser, that he had got it all wrong, and that the people who came to play here would always beat him.

They were sitting round the table now. They had been play-ing for nearly three hours, but it felt much longer. There was, Nick couldn't help but sense, a strangely oppressive atmos-phere tonight, over and above the fact that they were at his house. He checked his cards again, well aware that he'd only just looked: the four of spades and the eight of diamonds. Well, that was nothing to get worked up about, but he needed to play it, he needed to start winning some money back. Who knows, he might also win back some dignity and self-respect as well.

'Three pounds,' said Vijay.

'Call,' said Alan.

'Sounds like a reasonable bet,' said Doug.

'Call,' said Nick.

'Call three pounds,' said Simon.

Of course, it was possible that he wasn't all that bad at poker. It was even possible that he was quite a good player.

Maybe he had just been really unlucky, and maybe Doug had just been really lucky for all these months. He couldn't believe that he was actually a terrible player – no, for all his problems, he wasn't as unlucky as all that. But it was mystifying – the way that the same people kept winning and the same people kept losing, almost as if they deserved to.

The flop was dealt on to the table. Up came the four of hearts, the seven of clubs and queen of diamonds. Well, that meant he had a pair of fours at least. That should be worth sticking around for, but what were those other swine going to do?

'Three pounds,' said Vijay.

'Call,' said Alan.

'I'm happy with that,' said Doug.

'Call,' said Nick.

'Fold,' said Simon.

The fourth card came up. It was the eight of spades. Now this was even better – two pairs. Both cards in his hand had a match on the table. It was hard to believe that anyone had anything better than that, not the way they'd been betting. But he needed a big pot. It was important to make those bastards pay if they wanted to stay in for the final card.

'Two pounds,' said Vijay.

'Call,' said Alan.

'Call,' said Doug.

'Your two and raise eight pounds,' said Nick.

'Fold,' said Vijay.

'Fold,' said Alan.

'Well, I think it would be rude to leave our host on his own for this one,' said Doug, breezily throwing his chips into the pot.

Though, of course, the problems with Doug were not just limited to what he looked like, or every cretinous little thing he said every time he made a bet. There was also what he lived in. That bloody house. It was almost as problematic as the fact that he kept winning at poker. It was, without a doubt, the most ludicrous place he'd ever spent any time in. True, Nick would have loved to live there himself, but that only added to its ghastliness. All that money, all that space, all that conspicuous consumption. He didn't even know where to start: the double-panel oak front door, the vast lounge that could have so comfortably held the ProPokerPlus!, the lunatic portrait of the family in the hallway, the eerily oversized bathroom, with its sunken bath and perplexing contraptions. Well, the one good thing about playing at home was that it meant not playing there.

Simon dealt the final card. Nick looked in dismay. It was the queen of spades. The fucking queen of fucking spades, to go along with the queen of diamonds already on the table. Well, that was likely to change things, and not in a good way. Sure enough, that bastard Doug could hardly sit still. Two pairs wasn't so good if there was a higher pair already on the table, and it was no good at all if that cocksucker already had a queen in his hand.

'Bet ten pounds,' said Nick, not really sure what to do but desperate to get it over with as soon as possible.

'Oh I think we can make it more exciting than that, Mr Williams. Your ten and raise thirty,' said Doug.

What to do now? Was Doug bluffing, or did he really have another queen in his hand? Nick would never know. He shook his head sadly.

'No, fold. You can take it,' he said.

Beaming, Doug eagerly stretched his thick arms and dragged the chips back towards him. It was a large pot, there was nearly a hundred pounds in there, but he didn't take it all. For, there, left in the middle of the table, was a small pile of chips, about twenty pounds' worth. He looked at Nick with an imbecilic grin. The grin of an overfriendly ten-year-old boy, or perhaps one of those psychopathic prison guards that turn up in films and do foul things to people.

'You keep those, but don't play them – cash them in. Take Janet out to a restaurant or something. It would do you both good to eat out once in a while, to get out of this place.' As he said this, he swept his arm up in the air, but gesturing to what? It could be almost anything – the walls, the paintings, the poker table, the furniture, the floorboards, the window frames, his neighbours.

Nick stared at him in amazement. In the circumstances, in *any* circumstances, it was one of the most insulting things that Doug could have done. It was hard to imagine that he could have designed anything more cruel, more likely to hurt and humiliate. But did he design it? Was it a cold-blooded, cleverly constructed attempt to undermine him or was Doug just blundering around like a fucking pillock? Christ, maybe he was trying to be *kind*. Well, whatever his intentions, the result was the same. Nick had been fucked.

Nick didn't say anything, and didn't look at anyone else – he was furious with them as well. Not one of those spineless fucks had even said anything, though if any one of them dared to intervene on his behalf, they really would be in trouble. Nick raised a beer bottle to his lips. It was empty, but he pretended to drink from it anyway. There was an appalling silence, but alas Doug seemed determined to misinterpret it.

'As big as it is, even our place can get a bit much, so I try to take Sophia out once a fortnight. Treat her a bit. You should do the same. I know you don't have quite the same options round here, but you could go to that Chinese at the end of your road.'

'I think it's just a takeaway,' said Vijay.

Doug nodded. There was another silence, but now Nick couldn't look at Doug any more. He couldn't hold his gaze, not any longer, his eyes were getting wet. Oh God, was he going to start *crying*, of all things? That was the danger when you'd had too much to drink, and were getting publicly humiliated. He stared down at a spot on the ProPokerPlus!, clenched his jaw and wished for them all to fuck off. Simon shuffled and dealt the cards. There was an hour left to play.

Nick stayed up late that night, gloomily staring over the debris of another highly unsuccessful poker evening. It wasn't just the psychological damage, that at least he could afford, but it was also so bloody expensive. He had declared his total losses to Vijay at eighty pounds, but it may even have been double that. He had drunk so much that he couldn't recall with certainty how much money he had cashed in, and now he was too frightened to. Vijay must have guessed. He had been increasingly under-declaring his losses for months now. He was going to need *another* fucking bank loan, and for how long could he keep it from Janet? It was hopeless: even his lies were becoming unsustainable. Plus some wanker, almost certainly himself, had managed to spill a glass of red wine over the table. Any more spillages and the ProPokerPlus! would not just be a hugely expensive joke but also, like his paintings, worthless.

It was at this point that Nick had what he would later come to think of as his epiphany. He needed something to do. He had turned forty, he didn't like his job, he didn't have any children, he didn't really have any hobbies, except poker and the internet, and he was hardly likely to experiment with home improvements again. He needed a project – something to fill his fifth decade with and give some purpose to his life. And now he knew, with a startling vividness, what it would be.

He would fuck Doug. Doug was a monster and had to be destroyed, and he would be the one to do it. Nick understood immediately and clearly what the role entailed – after all, it was firmly within the literary canon. Doug was Grendel, the Minotaur, Sauron, Goldfinger and he, Nick, would be Beowulf, Theseus, Frodo, James Bond. It would be a heroic act. He would do it for moral reasons, to rid the world of a great evil. He would do it because of Sophia, though he still wasn't sure if he wanted to save her from Doug or destroy her as well. He would do it because it would make him feel good about himself, and most of all he would do it for the others – for Vijay, for poor Alan and for Simon, though that wouldn't preclude him from possibly having to fuck them over at some point in the future as well.

Nick wasn't mad – he wasn't going to kill Doug or physically assault him or anything. That really would be risky, and with something like this it was vital to maintain the moral high ground. There was no need to anyway. No – all that Nick needed to do was beat him at cards. That didn't mean having the odd good evening once in a while at his expense. That meant *beating him up at cards* – thrashing him, demeaning him at the table, inflicting a devastating loss, or perhaps a series of huge defeats, all so heavy and spirit-crushing that Doug retired from playing cards for good. He would make Doug experience what he himself had been put through tonight, but with a violence and horror that would be utterly, possibly even unjustly, disproportionate.

Of course, he could never hope to impoverish him or anything – that only happened in films, and no one was going to play for that kind of money. Also it had to be borne in mind that what Doug would regard as a moderately serious financial blow would be a total fucking catastrophe for him. But that wasn't the point. Nick wasn't stupid, and whatever Vijay may think, they didn't play poker for money. They played poker to hurt one another, and sometime in the near future Nick was going to cripple Doug. He would make it happen. The only question now was how.

Round at Vijay's – April

The one thing his spreadsheets made clear, abundantly clear, was that at least one of the others was lying. They had to be. Whatever else it might be, poker was a zero-sum game. All winnings minus all losses equals zero. The sum of the winnings must exactly equal the sum lost. They had to. This simple arithmetical rule was one of the many things he loved about the game. So why didn't his spreadsheets add up? Why? Because people were lying, that was why. They could hardly be making errors – not every single month, and anyway surely no one ever really miscounted how much they'd won or lost at poker. So the question was – were Simon and Doug exaggerating their winnings, or were Nick and Alan under-reporting their losses? And was it just one of them? Maybe all of them were lying except him? It was by no means impossible – he had thought deeply about it, as he did with most things, and could see motives on all sides.

One *could* say, he supposed, that it was just another form of bluffing, but after much consideration he had rejected this line of argument. Vijay was an accountant, which meant that he worked within rather than outside the law, and the distinction between tax avoidance and tax evasion was dear to him. People could bluff as much as they liked in the game, but they shouldn't do so when they weren't playing. All right, perhaps, it wasn't quite cheating, but to lie to a spreadsheet, not to mention a spreadsheet belonging to a chartered accountant, was disrespectful to say the least.

'Three pounds,' said Nick.

'Call,' said Simon.

'I'm good for three,' said Doug.

'Call,' said Alan.

'Call,' said Vijay.

He had the seven and eight of clubs. More than enough to play with, but he didn't see any reason to push it at this stage. Doug or Simon would doubtless have done something a bit more aggressive, and Nick something incredibly stupid, but Vijay was different. He was a careful player. Not fearful or overdefensive like Alan, but he did like to think about his bets. He may not know much about cards or card players, and human psychology wasn't something that he had ever taken an interest in, but he did know about money. He respected money, he understood it without ever loving or fearing it. And no wonder – he had, after all, dedicated most of his life to thinking about it.

Down came the flop. On the table was the ten of clubs, the two of diamonds and the jack of hearts. Now this could be interesting. The flush was still a possibility of course, though the odds of the next two cards coming up clubs was no more than four per cent; the straight was much more likely – though still the odds were no higher than seventeen per cent. The *straight flush* was even possible, though that of course was just a fraction of a percentage and should be discounted – in all the time they had been playing, he had never seen one. A flush or a straight would almost certainly win him the hand, but other than that he had nothing – no pairs, no back-up. One would have to assume that someone else would have at least something. So, say, a twenty per cent chance of having the best hand. He had to think some more about this.

'Five pounds,' said Nick.

'Call five pounds,' said Simon.

'Not this time,' said Doug, shaking his head.

'Call,' said Alan.

One of the things that always amazed Vijay about his friends was how quickly they were able to make their bets! Were they geniuses or morons? Surely they couldn't all be calculating the odds in this time. Not Nick or Doug, surely? And if they weren't, then what were they doing betting? Vijay hated being rushed but, as so often, time was running out. They were waiting for him. There was more than forty pounds already in the pot, so staying in for a further five didn't seem unreasonable. OK, so be it – for now.

'Call five pounds,' said Vijay, but he wasn't entirely comfortable with this.

The fourth card came up. The three of clubs! Well, well. The straight was looking less likely now, but the flush was still very much alive. Even so, one mustn't get carried away at this point. The probability of that final card coming up clubs was twenty per cent, the chances of it being the nine he needed for the straight were nine per cent. So, he now had approximately a thirty per cent chance of producing a winning hand. And what about the others? Since the great disaster at Doug's two months ago, he was all too aware that there could be another, better flush out there. But it was only now that he started to look at his companions.

He must have been looking a bit too hard, because Simon suddenly jerked his head forward and stuck out his tongue. Vijay laughed cautiously, carefully watching the others to check whether it actually was a joke. With Simon it could sometimes be hard to tell. With Doug of course it was easy, because he always laughed as well, and Nick made lots of jokes, but no one was ever expected to laugh at them, so that was OK. Alan never made any jokes, so that was all right too – but Simon was an odd one. Did he even like playing with them? It was hard to tell with Simon what he might like or dislike. Another, related, mystery was why no one seemed to like Doug very much, even though he was easily the most generous host, who always offered a wide range of alcoholic and non-alcoholic drinks, and the very best in the way of hot and cold snacks.

Vijay only stored wins and losses on his spreadsheets, but he noted and remembered much more than this. He was an accountant by upbringing, training, instinct and socio-ethnic stereotype. He had noted for example that the supermarket pizzas provided by Nick were of a particularly cheap brand, that the corn chips were sometimes soft and that the hummus and salsa dips had on more than one occasion been past their sell-by dates. Although he had to acknowledge that there was always plenty to drink round at Nick's, and it was altogether better than at Simon's, where the hospitality was, if not ungenerous, then certainly uncompromising – red wine, crackers and goat's cheese, and nothing other than tap water if you wanted a soft drink.

But for a more meaningful comparison, Doug's generosity had to be set against levels of income and wealth, and so Vijay had gone to the trouble to work out how much they all earned. It didn't take long. Nick was a secondary-school teacher with no managerial responsibilities and earned twenty-eight thousand three hundred and fifty pounds a year. Simon was a lecturer at the University of Reading and so on his current salary band it wasn't possible for him to earn more than thirty-seven thousand five hundred pounds. Vijay's firm did the accounts for where Alan worked and so that was easy

– he was paid fifty-seven thousand pounds with benefits and a discretionary annual bonus of up to ten per cent. Vijay himself had earned seventy-one thousand three hundred and forty-five pounds last year, though by making use of tax allowances he was able to take home a higher proportion of this than the others – something that had to be judiciously weighed against the fewer days they worked, and the intangible benefits of working in state education, one of the few subjects that Vijay had developed strong views on.

But how much did Doug earn – that was the real question! How much did he *really* earn? Vijay very much wanted to be his accountant, if only to know for sure. Was it a hundred thousand a year or three hundred thousand – somewhere in between, he guessed, but he couldn't know. Even more difficult was how much he was worth. His total net-asset wealth, what was it – two, three million? It couldn't be any more than that, surely? Of course, a man like Doug employed his own accountants in order to stop accountants like Vijay, particularly the ones at the Inland Revenue, from ever being able to find out. Doug was unusually reticent about this side of his business affairs, but he had given enough away for Vijay to suspect that he was doing all the right things – his wife on the payroll, relations and in-laws holding a range of mysterious directors' posts, a holding company based on the island of Jersey. And if there was one thing he knew about Doug, then it was how much he hated paying tax. It was a constant theme to their conversations – indeed, it was largely how they had become friends in the first place. Well, at least he didn't have to pay any tax on his poker winnings.

'Two pounds,' said Nick.

'Call,' said Simon.

'Your two and raise five,' said Alan.

So Alan had something. But what? Vijay knew this wasn't what he was good at. He was much more confident working out what kind of hand he might be able to make than what kind of hand the others had. Although, this time round, it wasn't so very hard. Alan wouldn't bet like this unless he already had something quite good – two pairs, or maybe even three of a kind. Given the cards on the table, it wasn't possible for him to have a flush or straight already, and if he was staying in order to make one of those, then he would want to keep the betting as low as possible. Pleased with his reasoning so far, he now had to decide what he was going to do himself. It wasn't so difficult. He had roughly a thirty per cent chance to win this, and there was nearly sixty pounds in the pot, so a seven-pound bet would give him a return of more than eight to one.

'Call seven pounds,' said Vijay.

'Fold,' said Nick.

'Fold,' said Simon.

'Call,' said Alan.

The final card was dealt. It was the ace of hearts. A strong card, but no good at all – not to him at least. Whether it was any use to Alan or not was largely irrelevant, for Alan almost certainly had him beaten anyway.

'Bet ten pounds,' said Alan.

'Fold,' said Vijay.

And that was that. Alan was clearly delighted but Vijay was reasonably happy as well. Poker, like so much else, was a long-term undertaking, which meant that it was the process more than the results that mattered. It was like a financial audit – whatever the business, whatever the balance sheets, it was the process that had to be followed. And Vijay had followed the process expertly, his analysis had been correct and his calculations accurate. It was just the outcome that hadn't been any good on this occasion. But it would on others; it would on many others.

*   *   *

Of all the houses they played at, Alan liked Vijay's the best. Or rather, and it amounted to the same thing, it was the one where he felt least uncomfortable. Doug's was the grandest, of course, and he hated it. Nick tried to do his best, but unfortunately his house was horrible and ever since he had got that new table it had become terribly cramped. It didn't help that Alan's car had once been broken into when parked outside and he always took that kind of thing badly. Ever since then he had found himself fidgeting even more than usual, and checking at the window every half-hour. Even Simon's flat was probably better – an appalling mess of course, with newspapers, books and papers and half-empty cups of coffee all carelessly moved from the table on to the sofa, chairs and floor moments before they arrived. Everything Simon owned was so appallingly *old* – the hilarious record player, the discontinued make of desktop computer, the faded sofa with the unreliable arms. Thank goodness Alan wasn't a member of the bohemian middle classes if that's what they had to put up with.

Vijay's house was far from perfect. It was slightly too warm and when you first came in it smelt strongly of pineapple deodoriser. The lumpy kids were a nuisance – spoilt by Vijay and overdisciplined by Sarita, they never went to bed on time and would come hurtling down to the table to ask for sweets. Plus at some point in the evening there was usually a difficult moment when he and Sarita could be heard shouting at one another in Punjabi in the kitchen, and the others would have to exchange awkward semi-amused glances.

But the positives were considerable. Unlike Doug's, this was not a house designed to impress Reading's business class – in fact it clearly hadn't been designed at all. Even Alan, who struggled to make assessments on this kind of thing, could tell that. As a consequence, it was comfortable and welcoming, and happily reminded him of the common room at his old university's computer science department. Characterised not by an abundance of space, like Doug's, but by *things*, it was actually nearly as big as Doug's, but seemed much smaller and friendlier, what with all the stuff piled up everywhere. Wherever you were, you could be sure there would be a soft foam chair, a small table, an audio-visual device, a rug, some pretty but not very helpful cushions, something to trip over and something oriental and curious to pick up and puzzle over.

And then there was Sarita's cooking. Everything fried in clever spices and too much butter, and extravagantly piled up just like the furniture. It was like being at one of those tandoori restaurants on London Road with their all-you-can-eat buffet deals. No wonder Vijay was so overweight. Well, at least Alan didn't have to worry about *that*. One of the good things about worrying about everything else was that he had the kind of overactive metabolism and excessive twitching and sweating which was guaranteed, no matter how much he ate, to always keep him looking thin, malnourished and faintly unwell.

'Two pounds,' said Nick.

'Call,' said Vijay.

'Not for me,' said Doug.

'Call,' said Simon.

Alan thought for a moment. He had been dealt a pair of kings, which meant that he had almost certainly been given the burden of having the best hand. Without any great relish, he had felt obliged to open the betting with something appropriately bold, but now they'd had the flop and on the table now, giving him no help at all, was the five of spades, the four of clubs and the queen of hearts.

Now what? It seemed his only viable strategy was to bluff. To convince the others that that pile of shit served up in front of them was somehow exactly what he had wanted. Maybe they'd think he had a pair of queens, and was now sitting there with three. Whatever, the vital thing now was to show that he was seriously expecting to win this hand, that he wasn't a frightened rabbit and he wasn't some hopeless schmuck who had got out of his depth – he was a poker player, and when he was given a big hand like this he used it to make as much money as possible.

Trying to sound as confident as he could, he announced in what was possibly too loud a voice, 'Meet the two pounds, and raise another seven.'

Nick folded straight away and then Vijay, more slowly, shook his head and did the same. As usual, Nick had just been hanging in there hopefully, but almost certainly Vijay had been sitting on a more promising hand, maybe the makings of a run. So his bluff was working – he felt a little surge of excitement. He was reading their hands expertly, he was betting with courage and precision. Maybe, at long last, he was getting good at this game.

But no, of course not. It was never going to be that simple. For now it had got round to Simon, who was looking at him closely. There was a significant pause. Alan disliked being scrutinised by anyone but particularly by Simon. Who wouldn't? He wasn't large and formidable like Doug – he didn't lean over and look him up and down dramatically. Instead he sat back, with his evil and penetrating stare and cold, inhuman intelligence. Simon had horrible eyes. Pale blue, he supposed you'd have to call them, but they were colourless really, like glass, eyes that looked but could never be looked into. And, as always when this happened, Alan immediately started worrying about his tell.

A 'tell' is a physical signal given unconsciously at times of stress. It is associated with attempting to lie or otherwise deceive someone, as in a game of poker. They had been playing for twelve months before Doug patiently explained the concept to Alan and then, alarmingly, told him that he had one. Although he wouldn't, of course, say what it was.

Alan had been paralysed with fear ever since. Thinking about it, it was completely obvious that he would have one. Just like being colour blind, being unable to pee in front of other men and suffering from eczema. Of course he would have a tell. But what the hell was it? He had scoured the psychological literature and it had soon become apparent that a tell could be absolutely anything – anything at all. Some people played with their hair, others cracked their knuckles or ground their teeth or bit their fingers, some unfortunates belched involuntarily or picked their noses or reached down to touch their crotches, and lots fiddled with their wrist-watches, poker chips, rings and jewellery. And, amazingly, *none of them knew they were doing it!* That was the true horror of the tell.

So what was it that he did? Well, he didn't wear any jewellery, but he did wear glasses. Those were a clear risk. Did he touch them, push them back on to his sweating nose, or play with their arms? He had spent a great deal of time staring into the mirror at home. He had even asked Alice to watch him carefully over dinner, but that was no good, of course – Alice was just about the only person in the world he *didn't* get self-conscious in front of. The whole point of the tell was that it only emerged at moments of pressure and tension – when he was being scrutinised and tested, examined and doubted. At moments exactly like this.

There weren't any rules about how long you had to take to bet. Maybe it would be a good idea to have some. Alan was starting to construct some sort of suitably polite prompt, when Simon quietly said, 'OK, I'll call your seven pounds.'

So Simon was staying in. Now what? He had to carry on with his bluff, that's what. But what about his tell? Whatever it was, it was now almost certainly enormous and grotesque, a flashing red bulb on his nose. Alan's nose had always been problematic. It seemed that the one element of his crypto-Jewish lineage to reveal itself was not an exceptional talent for classical music or disarming social confidence, but rather his appalling nose – a fleshy, overripe thing that curiously looked as if it was made of muscle rather than cartilage, and which bulged jarringly, idiotically, over his narrow face.

Nick dealt another card on to the table – an eight of clubs. No good to him, but possibly very helpful for Simon if he was trying to build a straight. On the other hand, there were no pairs show-ing on the table. There was every chance that Simon had nothing winnable as yet, was staying in order to make a hand, rather than because he had one. In which case Alan could maybe still drive him out. He filled his mouth with beer. His hands were wet and his mouth was dry. Maybe that was his tell? Is that what he did every time he was bluffing? Did his mouth dry up and he took a drink? Christ, this was torture. And to think he did this every month because it was meant to be fun – a hobby. He didn't do hill walking, water sports or tennis. He didn't follow football or have a pub-quiz team. This was all he had, his one leisure activity. No wonder he was so bloody depressed.

It was his bet. Now, tell or no tell, he had to get this just right. He had to appear so ridiculously confident, so absent-mindedly, happily at ease with himself that Simon got the message – fuck off. Just drop your cards and fuck off, you fucker. But appearing confident and carefree wasn't some-thing Alan had ever found easy at the best of times. Trying to do it now, with Simon's eyes of death on him and this braying bunch of idiots goggling at them both was to all intents and purposes impossible.

'Raise twelve pounds,' said Alan, staring determinedly at a spot on the ceiling.

'Call,' said Simon immediately, barely even looking up.

And on they went again. Before he could stop himself, he'd had *another* gulp of beer. In normal circumstances, he rarely drank. So that had to be the tell, or was it his nose after all, or his glasses, or the sudden urge he had to touch his crotch? He knew that he was, in just about every sense, falling apart.

The last card came down. The jack of diamonds. No good, of course, but unlikely to be much good for Simon either. Or was it? Maybe it was exactly what he'd wanted. It was impossible to know. For the whole hand, he had sat back in his seat, as impassive as ever. Alan, meanwhile, was now shaking. But surely that wasn't the tell, he didn't usually shake, did he? Surely that had to be just an ancillary symptom.

So, at last, the final round of betting. It was the biggest pot of the night and there was considerable, hugely unwelcome interest from the others. Vijay was rubbing his hands excitedly: there was nothing he liked more than watching this kind of thing. Nick was looking happier than he'd done all evening, delighted that for once he wasn't the one in this mess. Doug had returned from the kitchen with more beers and was still standing, making occasional moronic whooping noises. Alan's principal interest was now no longer winning the hand so much as losing with the minimum degree of humiliation. He had to bet something – that was obvious. Of course, the most cost-effective thing to do would be to check, wait for Simon to put in a bet and fold. But the obvious problem with this strategy was that he would look like the most incredible fool. No, he had to see it through. It was expensive, it was illogical, it was self-destructive. But the truth was, he wasn't brave enough to let the others think he was a coward.

'Twenty pounds,' he said casually. He wasn't sure where he should be looking. If he looked down, didn't that show he was scared; if he looked up, wouldn't it mean he was lying? But it would be foolhardy to actually stare into Simon's eyes. They were wicked and frightening, and almost certainly hypnotic. He would fall under his spell.

This time Simon paused. Alan had at the very least given him something to think about. And, for the first time, he leant forward ever so slightly to have a closer look at him. There was silence round the table – even Doug had shut up. The tell, whatever it was, could now be doing anything. Alan decided to stay as still as possible. Like a small mammal in the jaws of a predator, he knew the best thing to do was to play dead. He put his hands on the table, where he could safely see them, and remained motionless. Instead of worrying about where his eyes should be, he tried to let them calmly glaze over. If anything, it was now Simon who seemed to be uncertain. He could sense him probing, furiously trying to work out what was going on. Alan tried to empty his mind, so that it couldn't be read. Isn't that what Buddhist monks did? It wasn't the kind of thing he knew much about, and this was hardly the time to learn. Instead he just imagined elderly Chinese men sitting by water pools, woodland glades and green meadows – anything that would radiate an inscrutable inner calm.

Simon gave a shallow yet distinct sigh. But not of satisfaction. Definitely not. It was a sigh of exasperation, possibly even resignation. He was on the verge of giving up – yes, Simon was giving up! He had slunk back again in his chair now, disengaging, taking his vile eyes away. The bluff, the most spectacular that Alan, and maybe anyone else, had ever made, was working! All he had to do was just stay calm for a few moments longer and it would all be over.

'Call,' said Simon.

He said it so gently that Alan didn't hear him properly at first. He had even for a moment thought that he'd folded, that he had done exactly what he had given every indication of doing just moments before. But no, he'd been called, and Simon was now looking at him not with suspicion, but with increasing confidence. The game was up. The bluff had failed, and he had no choice but to lay down his cards.

'I've got a pair of kings,' said Alan.

The room erupted. Doug started whooping again and slapping him vigorously on the back. There were general exclamations of surprise and delight. Vijay seemed especially pleased. Nick was shaking his head in wonder and possibly admiration. Alan had never felt so loved around the table. Of course, that was mainly because he had just lost a huge sum of money. Simon had a straight, and was dragging towards him the pile of chips. But whatever the financial loss, Alan had won their affection. Everyone loves an unsuccessful bluffer, and he had just attempted one of the biggest ever. It had very nearly worked too. Even Simon was looking at him with something approaching respect, saying nice things about how well he had played the hand and recalibrating his opinion of Alan for future rounds. It was quite probably the greatest single moment Alan had had in three years of playing poker – it was just a shame that he had hated every second of it, and that it had cost him more than a hundred pounds.

Nick had had a frustrating evening. He had watched Alan's unravelling in disgust and pity and was very glad to have missed out on that particular disaster, but there was little else to console him. He had ended the night seventy-five pounds down, which was hardly his greatest loss, in fact by recent standards it would have to count as something of a triumph, but he had made no progress at all with his project to destroy Doug. He was beginning to realise that it wasn't going to be as straightforward as he had first hoped. He had spent much of the evening trailing him, folding if Doug wasn't staying in, ramping up the betting if Doug looked like he was going to keep going to the end, but this was hardly a strategy for bringing Doug to his knees. All he'd done was fruitlessly and expensively play hands he shouldn't have. He hadn't even irritated him – if Doug had noticed anything at all about Nick's behaviour this evening, it would have been that he kept losing money to him in pointless ways.

No, a great deal more was required. Doug was his enemy now, and an enemy, he had to acknowledge this, was a term of respect. Defeating him would require entirely new levels of thought and dedication. He needed to go about things scientifically. He needed to manufacture a situation in which he was betting very large amounts of money against Doug, in the certain knowledge that he would beat him. What he needed to do was cheat.

Round at Simon's – May

As far as Simon could tell, and he hadn't made an exhaustive study, there were four main ways in which one could cheat at poker.

First, and most obviously, there was looking at another player's cards. He had only done this on a couple of occasions, and if pressed he would still maintain that it had been hard not to. He had been sitting next to Nick, who had been spastically drunk and kept waving his cards in front of him. True, he hadn't gone to the trouble of warning Nick that he could see them, but it seemed to Simon that looking at someone's cards and not looking *away* from someone's cards were very different things indeed, whatever some of his consequentialist philosopher colleagues might think.

He would have to acknowledge that he was on more shaky ground when he had experimented, albeit just the once, with a mirror. A little face mirror craftily placed in the corner of his sitting room, resting casually on a bookshelf and tilted down on to the table. It was, he thought, a subtle first attempt, which if anyone did spot (and they didn't, of course) he could have passed off wittily and easily. But it had been no better than a qualified failure. The others may not have been much good at poker, but they weren't complete fools. They looked at their two hidden cards carefully, lifting the cards only slightly up from the table, and there they remained. The only one who held his cards up to his face to read them was that idiot Nick, and the only one who ever forgot what cards he was holding and went back to check repeatedly was, of course, Nick again. So provided Nick was sitting with the mirror behind him, Simon was able, on occasion, to get a flash of what he was holding, but it was no more than that – at best, he could just about identify the colour of the suit or whether it was a picture card. But it was rather a pointless exercise – in general, the one person's hand he didn't need to know was Nick's.

Second, there was card marking. What a glorious prospect this was. To know each and every round, each and every card your opponents were holding! But it was also extremely difficult. Getting some sort of rudimentary marked set wouldn't be too hard, he supposed – that was pretty much the sort of thing the internet was invented for. But then you'd have to go to the trouble of learning the markings, and be able to read them across the table. This, it seemed, was far from straightforward. Not easy to master when they tended to play under soft lighting, and it wouldn't do to be squinting the whole time. He'd read that the way to do it now was with invisible, ultraviolet markings that could only be seen if one was wearing specially tinted contact lenses. But that sounded expensive and really all a bit much. Besides, he could hardly start insisting that they only use his pack of cards – that really would arouse suspicions, even with this lot, and the consequences of getting caught would be frightful.

Then there was crooked dealing. To ensure that one had the winning hand was, he supposed, the holy grail of cheating. Certainly it would be the most lucrative. The trick, of course, was not only to deal oneself the strongest hand, but also to deal someone else, preferably Doug, an exceptionally good one as well. This was really the stuff of film – where you dealt your enemy four aces and he bankrupted himself against your straight flush. But how many times could you get away with a stunt like that?

In any case, after downloading a pamphlet on the subject and two afternoons of semi-dedicated effort, he'd reached the conclusion that he simply couldn't do it. As one might have guessed, false dealing was far from easy. It was conjuring really, and it required nimble hands and quick, rather than contemplative, cognition. He was a philosophy lecturer. He was good at propositional logic, at devising and critiquing thought experiments, at scrutinising contradictions in complex abstract arguments. What he wasn't good at, what he had spent his entire adult life trying to avoid, was skilled manual labour.

Finally there was collusion with one or more fellow players. This seemed to offer less ambitious but still intriguing possibilities. To begin with, one could minimise losses if one knew exactly what one's partner was holding, but more interestingly there would be the scope to set traps, to stupidly, brazenly ratchet up the bidding and pull in the others, in the knowledge that it was one's partner, rather than oneself, who actually held the winning hand. Could it work? Simon would have loved to give it a try.

But in practice this didn't seem very plausible either. Who would he collude with? Vijay would barely even understand the question, and neither he nor Alan had anything like the imagination required. Just broaching the subject with either of them would be an ordeal that Simon wasn't prepared for. Nick would probably be up for it, in fact Nick would definitely be up for it, but he was just about the least reliable person that Simon had ever met. For it to work, collusion would require a level of ability way beyond Nick's, and he would almost certainly give it away with some God-awful blunder or drunken spectacular. No, the only remotely realistic candidate was unfortunately Doug, who just about had the commensurate skill, but probably not the appetite. He was a bruiser, no doubt about it, but this was unlikely to be his kind of thing. Raising it with him would be highly awkward, potentially disastrous, and since Alan and Nick lost all the time anyway, it didn't seem particularly profitable to risk things by ganging up on them.

So despite his investigations Simon had never bothered with cheating. Had anyone else? Like other people he knew who were interested in cheating, he had a phobia of being cheated himself. But there were no obvious suspects. Vijay – absolutely not. Alan – no. Nick almost certainly must have thought about it, but would obviously have been caught by now. Doug? Well, it would certainly help to explain why he was so successful despite being so intellectually stunted, but it was unlikely. Doug had a sportsman's ethics and world view, which tended to be strong on well-established, if philosophically problematic, rules of conduct around fair play, letting the best man win and doing the right thing. Doug undoubtedly fiddled his taxes and ripped off his customers, for all Simon knew he had a dozen mistresses and beat his children, but he probably wouldn't cheat at cards.

'Check,' said Alan.

'Three pounds,' said Nick.

'Call,' said Simon.

'I'm happy with that,' said Doug.

'Call,' said Vijay.

'Fold,' said Alan.

Vijay dealt the flop: the ten of diamonds, the four of clubs, the ten of spades. Now this was promising. Simon had the ten of clubs to match the two on the table, and the ace of hearts.

Three of a kind – good enough to win most hands, but there was always a chance that someone had it as well. Doug was still grinning stupidly – did he have the other ten, or was he just happy to be playing?

Simon didn't enjoy poker night as much as the others. This was largely because his reasons for playing were different and also, he suspected, highly unusual – Simon played poker in order to make money. It was depressing, it was actually faintly embarrassing for someone in his forties, but there was no getting away from it: he needed the income. What he *didn't* need was what all the others seemed so badly to want from poker night – an evening away from the wife, a sense of camaraderie and social bonding, a little bit of gentle taboo-breaking. Well, whatever it was for them, it was undoubtedly a nice little earner for him. He aimed to make one hundred pounds each evening and usually he made more. Eleven or twelve times a year and that made it almost fifteen hundred pounds tax free. It paid for his summer holiday and two months' mortgage repayment. Although he was well aware that he lived in a society unable to distinguish the difference between want and need, that hadn't stopped these poker evenings from becoming essential.

Of course, not long after he had started playing with them, he had begun looking for another game. Another, wealthier set, where people played just as artlessly but with much more money. Where he didn't have to sit in cramped suburban kitchens or squashed behind Nick's absurd table in that odious living room, or in Doug's appalling house, drinking bottles of supermarket beer and wine from a box.

But years of searching had convinced him that the sucker that everyone dreamt of didn't exist, not in real life. The dim-witted, drunken young millionaire Duke who would happily sit down for a game of cards and think nothing of losing ten thousand pounds. It was a recognisable literary type but not, alas, a sociological one. People were rich not just because they were good at making money, but also because they were good at holding on to it. The English aristocracy had gone on for centuries steadily accumulating wealth, yes, exploiting rural labourers and tenant farmers and the proletariat and everyone else – yes, yes, doubtless. But more importantly, they hadn't lost it. *That* was their true genius. They hadn't let their sons and daughters marry penniless oiks, they hadn't let themselves be robbed by Communist revolutionaries, and they hadn't sat down to games of poker and risked everything they owned on the turn of a card. Or at least not with him they hadn't. As far as Simon could tell, the only people that rich people ever lost money to were other rich people.

Not that Simon hadn't tried. Two years ago he had wriggled his way into some games in London. Big-money games, where they won and lost hundreds of pounds, not over the course of the night, but in a single hand. It had been a chastening experience. The money was there all right, and the apartments they played in had been just what he had expected – generously proportioned and uncluttered, with impressive, uncomfortable furniture and dizzying views over the Thames. The table had been just like poor Nick's, though here they could all sit round it comfortably in the middle of the room, without their backs squeezed against the wall, and they played with exactly the same chips that Doug had – chunky composite-clay chips, which felt good in the fist of the hand, and landed on the table with a soft thud.

But the businessmen he played against hadn't been fat or greedy or stupid, and the young bankers hadn't been reckless or drug-addled. All they drank was sparkling water, and to his immense disappointment they were unnervingly good at poker. They didn't play like him and they certainly didn't play like the others. There were no theatricals – no side talk, no eye rolling, no badly executed jokes. They didn't make brainless attempts to intimidate him. They didn't closely scrutinise him, they didn't try to hold his gaze or bore into his head. They hardly even looked at him. Instead, they just folded or bet – swiftly, quietly, with precision and verve.

They had brilliant stamina. They played until late into the night, and there was no stopping to eat pizzas or smoke or drink beer or talk about football or complain about their wives. All they did, for hour after hour, was play poker. Did they enjoy it? Maybe, in the same way that Simon had once liked playing chess. It was, he supposed, stimulating and, unlike him, they didn't need the money, so he supposed it would have to be classified as a leisure activity. But they didn't seem to be having a particularly good time.

The first time he played continuously for six hours and finished, dry-throated and drained and with a vile headache, up by three pounds fifty. The next time he lost four hundred pounds. It was easily the biggest loss of his life. He felt nauseous, wounded, as if he had been assaulted. He had driven back home in a daze, disorientated and a little bit tearful. When he at last reached home, at 5 a.m., just as the first light of a summer's morning was trickling through the windows, he had climbed into his bed fully clothed, and wrapped himself beneath the unlaundered covers, his head pressed under the pillow. He wanted dark and silence, and to smell nothing other than himself. He wanted, more than anything else, to feel safe again.

Sloshing around in his head, beneath the shock and horror and the sick-making ghastliness of losing so much money, was the sad realisation that he wasn't good enough. He had reached as far as his ambition and skill and nerve would ever take him, and he would have to learn to make do with what he had. It would take three months of playing mercilessly in Reading to make up the loss from that one night. And he had never played a big-money game again.

So Simon would have to content himself with winning money from people who weren't rich and whom he knew and trusted, and who weren't that good at poker. Whether you were predator or, in his case, parasite, the secret of survival was not to be the fastest or the strongest, but the best adapted – to fit into your surroundings, to exploit efficiently what was available. He had found his ecological niche. It wasn't the most productive of niches, he felt cramped, frustrated by the obvious limits of its resources and opportunities, but it was undeniably his and it was stable and it was sustainable.

'Five pounds,' said Nick.

'Not for me,' said Doug.

'Call,' said Vijay.

Now this was surprising. Of course, nearly everything Nick did was surprising, but it was odd that both of them were going in at five pounds – particularly Vijay. Maybe he did have the other ten? Even so, Simon still had the ace, so he should get this. Unless, of course, one of them was on for a full house. But they were unlikely to have it yet. Maybe he should drive them out now to be sure? But no, it would be nice to push this one just a bit further.

'Call,' said Simon.

Up came the next card, but Simon wasn't looking at it just yet. Whatever it was, it wasn't going to go anywhere, and he was more interested for the moment in what the others made of it. The answer was not very much by the looks of things. Never one to hide his feelings when it mattered most, Nick looked thoroughly pissed off. As for Vijay, well, he wasn't the type of player to pull faces, but there had been the tiniest flicker of something there, a spasm of disappointment, maybe even irritation, before his usual placid cheeriness had returned.

When he did look down, he saw that the card was the five of clubs. Would be handy for anyone trying to make a straight, but surely none of them had been seriously looking for that? And if Nick now wanted to spend more money foolishly trying to beat the odds and get one, well, he'd better make sure it was as expensive as possible for him.

'Two pounds,' said Nick.

OK, that was what Simon would have expected. Nick hadn't actually checked, but clearly he didn't want the bidding to get too aggressive. Which meant of course that it was time to get aggressive.

'Call two pounds,' said Vijay.

So neither of them had the stomach for it, which meant neither of them had the cards. Well, this was going to be easy. The only questions were whether he brought this to an end now or not, and, if he did let them have another chance, how much they would have to pay for it.

'Your two, and raise another eight,' said Simon.

'Call,' said Nick.

There was a pause, and Simon patiently waited for Vijay to do his calculations. It was, he knew, no good rushing him.

'Fold,' he said at last, and reluctantly. There had probably been half a good hand there.

The last card came out. The jack of diamonds. Well, unless Nick had something unexpected that wasn't going to do him any good. Nick being Nick, that wasn't of course impossible and it wouldn't be entirely out of keeping for him to have two jacks in his hand. There had been plenty of times when Nick had stayed in for round after round, doggedly and stupidly to the end, and then miraculously and idiotically pulled out the winning card. But of course, there had been many more times when he hadn't. Poker was, in many ways, essentially a dull game – especially if played well.

'One pound,' said Nick.

There were times when Simon almost felt sorry for him.

'Raise twenty pounds,' said Simon.

Nick shook his head. Simon pulled the pot towards him. Gosh, this was so *easy*. If only it was slightly more lucrative. If only poor Nick earned a little bit more, so he could afford to lose a little bit more money to him. If only Doug played poker like Nick. If only the *upper classes* played poker like Nick.

Although earning money was Simon's sole interest in playing poker, it hadn't always been the case. In fact, Simon had first started playing for a reason that had nothing to do with money – philosophy. It had been a long time ago, just after he had finished his doctorate and started lecturing in London. It had been the most creative and exciting time of his life, before propositional logic had exhausted him, epistemological scepticism had started to irritate him and metaphysics had defeated him. Back then, even the teaching didn't demoralise him. He had, and this was now barely credible, *liked* his students – he was interested in them, concerned for, if not their well-being, then at least their intellectual development. He actually wanted them to have a good education. He wanted them to challenge him, to help progress the subject, to seek out truths and dismantle falsehoods. He wanted them to like him.

He was helping to run a course in the philosophy of language for postgraduate students and, with the kind of enthusiasm and inventiveness that seemed so alien to him now, he had had the highly novel idea of using poker as a means of illustrating Wittgenstein's theory of language games. At the time, of course, he had been besotted with Wittgenstein. They all had been. He was, after all, the cleverest, most eccentric, unworldly, morally pure philosopher that ever lived. What

Simon had been *less* sure about was whether he had been right or not.

Imagine a game, a universe, a language system in which there were only four words, and that these four words provided all the information you ever needed to be able to interact and function. Wittgenstein had tried to do just that and hardly anyone had been sure what he was on about, but it turned out that he needn't have bothered; it turned out that there already was exactly such a system – poker. Just like in Wittgenstein's thought experiment, there were four words: call, raise, fold and check. In real poker you needed to have some numbers as well, but every communication, which meant every meaningful statement, was constructed from these words and these alone.

What did this mean? What were the implications of this? What did the word *call* actually correspond to? Was it a word at all, or was it a rule? Perhaps, as Wittgenstein maintained, words were rules, or at least had their rules embedded in them. And what would happen if someone used these words incorrectly – if someone said *raise* when they actually meant *fold*? Would it be legitimate to describe this as false, or would it just be meaningless? What grounds might there be for doubting someone's use of *check*? To what extent did the existence of the game of poker confirm Wittgenstein's refutation of Cartesian scepticism?

Delighted with his little conceit, Simon had soon started playing poker with the postgraduate students, and then teaching and playing it to his favourite undergraduates. It helped that every term they received generous grant awards, were naive about money and hopeless at poker. The students loved it, of course. When you are nineteen years old, losing money at cards is only marginally less thrilling than winning money at cards. Whether they actually learnt anything about

Wittgenstein's theory of language was more questionable. Certainly, to begin with, Simon would use every hand as an opportunity to explore and discuss its philosophical ramifications and their games would be punctuated by brilliant, crisp conversation, swoops of irony and powerful flourishes of logical reasoning. He had started to write a paper with the delightfully provocative title of 'Wittgenstein's Private Language Hypothesis and the Game of Poker – An Empirical Verification'. It was the late 1980s, he was the youngest and most fashionable philosopher in the department, and the postmodern daring of his poker experiments soon became a campus legend.

The years passed, and things changed. London was getting more expensive and vulgar, the University buildings more decrepit and overpopulated. Simon was getting older, the students more dopey and less entertaining. In fact, the only things that didn't seem to change were the problems of philosophy and his salary. A new Dean had started at the University and made it clear that he disapproved of members of staff gambling with students. Simon wasn't that bothered. It was 1995, he had been in London teaching the same subject for six years and he had lost interest in Wittgenstein. He never had got round to writing the paper on poker, and he couldn't remember why he had ever thought it a particularly good idea. He was starting to lose interest in many of the other things he had been doing as well and, besides, now that none of his students got grants any more, he wasn't making any money from them.

Not that he'd found any other way of making money since then. Simon was finally driven out of London by its cost and unending competitiveness, but his years as a wandering philosopher had scarcely been profitable ones. The lone scholars of medieval Europe had travelled from court to court, the honoured guests of popes and kings, making unverifiable pronouncements on the great issues of the day, instructing young princes in Aristotelian ethics, and initiating theological disputes that would send armies to battle halfway across the Continent. But in Southern England at the end of the twentieth century things had been rather different. It seemed that no one was particularly interested in philosophers any more and, to make matters worse, his expertise was on all the wrong things: British empiricism, David Hume, Bertrand Russell, logical positivism. It was hopeless – the only philosophers anyone was interested in learning about now were French and still alive. And so Simon had stumbled through a series of precarious positions: temporary tutoring contracts, maternity cover, external supervisions, part-time lectureships, one-year research grants that took six months to apply for – all badly paid and with appropriately low levels of prestige, security and status.

Finally, unexpectedly, he landed a job at the University of Reading, where he had to teach the ludicrous and ever popular introduction to modern philosophy course to a hundred second-year undergraduate students. They were appalling: their mobile phones kept going off in lectures, they insisted on speaking like African-Americans and were dreadful at logic. But he suspected they were no worse than any other Western adolescents and, besides, the main thing was that he had that rarest of philosophical phenomena – a permanent job. A job which wasn't very difficult, where no one expected him to write or say anything especially clever, and in which he only worked for eight months of the year. From time to time, they even paid for him to go to conferences in European cities, where he got to take drugs with other philosophers.

It was hardly Erasmus at the court of Henry VIII but, as with his card games, the job served him very well, and even if the world had lost interest in its philososophers, he hadn't yet lost interest in the world. He had even come to like Reading, with its robust commercialism and cheerful small-mindedness, and where over the years he had found all he had needed to make life civilised: a semi-reliable cannabis dealer, a high-quality wine merchant, and at least two perfectly respectable bookshops which let him buy on account. He liked his office on campus, where none of the students were ever interested or brave enough to bother him, and he had worked hard to develop a lasting appetite for the tomato soup and baked potatoes at the staff restaurant. But most of all, what he liked was his home – his beloved Georgian maisonette, the only property he had ever owned, and which was everything that Doug's wasn't: dignified, calmly lit, carefully proportioned, restful and elegantly faded. Simon himself hadn't faded – not completely, not yet, but he had reached the stage in life where it wasn't about wanting things any more, but about keeping them. He was determinded; he was quite prepared to be ruthless, about that. And that's where the poker came in.

Round at Doug's – June

Play the ball, not the man – one of those rules that every public schoolboy gets taught. A lesson for the rugby and cricket pitch, and with an obviously wider application. But what happens if the man has the ball? What if you very badly need to get it? And what if you never went to public school?

Nick feared and hated all sports, and he hated sportsmen with their cod ethics and infantile camaraderie and bogus sense of fair play. What did a twenty-two-year-old million-aire footballer know about fair play? And why should anyone be interested in his views on this or any other matter? Nick couldn't be sure, but he was pretty certain that he had been at least thirty-four years old before he said anything interesting. And yet, he had been disgusted to discover, on first entering the staff room, that his fellow teachers didn't do crosswords or discuss articles they'd read in the *London Review of Books*, but as likely as not would be talking about football. Worse, they would be talking about the *footballers* – not the matches or the referees or anything, but what the players, these adolescent numbskulls, were doing with their lives and cars and helicopters and girlfriends.

So fair play was out. Which was just as well, because it gave Nick a significant advantage over Doug. Doug was different from Nick – he *was* a sportsman, which meant that he did play by the rules. He played the ball. He played hard but played straight. In Doug's world, the best man won. But this wasn't Doug's world. This was poker, this was life: it was the man who won who was the best, and it didn't really matter how you went about it.

Given that Nick had been thinking about little else for the last six weeks, his plan was actually quite rudimentary. He was going to intimidate Doug. He was going to undermine him, freak him out, fuck him up, make him feel uncomfortable in himself, make him feel *bad* about himself. Since he was a Western male, it shouldn't be too difficult, it was just a matter of finding his weak spot. Obviously, Nick wasn't going to be able to intimidate Doug on the grounds of physical strength or wealth. But there were other things he could use. After all, that was what the class system was for.

'Your four, and raise another five pounds,' said Simon.

Things were going well. It was the first hand of the night, but already Nick had *drawn first blood* as sports commentators liked to say. It hadn't been difficult – for, to use another of those clunking sporting metaphors that were such a feature of just about anything Doug had ever said, he had provided Nick with something of an *open goal*.

In the front hallway, as they arrived, Doug had been proudly inviting them to inspect the McLain household's latest acquisition – a painting recently bought from a gallery in Windsor, and which Doug, unusually, had been allowed to choose as well as pay for. Nick's art-collecting days may have been over, but he of all people knew a calamity when he saw one, and he had immediately been overcome with joy by its awfulness.

It was a picture of a sprinter, tense and ready in a starting block, looking fiercely ahead, but the subject, predictable as it may have been, wasn't the problem. No, it was everything else that was so retarded, as if the last hundred years of art theory had never happened. Had the artist ever learnt anything other than how to paint? The naivety of the thing was breathtaking! The blockheaded attention to detail, the photographic realism and the cretinous airbrushing were sensational. It was hilariously, excitingly bad. And to Nick's astonishment and delight, Doug had paid more than four thousand pounds for it.

Nick didn't hold back. This was too good an opportunity and before he'd left home he had drunk two good, by which he meant large, glasses of white wine. He was feeling, as Doug would say, *on top of his game*, and he immediately launched into an incredible commentary on the painting, a brilliantly well-executed critique that went out of its way to congratulate Doug on having bought it, while at the same time making it clear that the painting was utterly without merit. Of course, Doug wouldn't have actually understood much of it and even Nick wasn't entirely sure what he was saying, but the subtext to his references to neo-impressionism, optic mixing and hypermodernism was beautifully clear: Doug knew nothing about art, he had terrible taste and had wasted a great deal of money.

'I'll call,' said Doug.

'Fold,' said Vijay.

'Fold,' said Nick.

Alan had already folded. And no wonder. Nick had noticed that the first round of the evening was often brisk. People were overoptimistic and overcaffeinated and it tended to show in their betting – his in particular. But tonight had been more ferocious than most. Was Doug rattled already? Whatever the reason, he was glad to get out of this one.

The fifth and final card was dealt on to the table. It was the queen of clubs, the highest card showing. There were no pairs, a flush was impossible, a straight highly improbable. If either of those two actually had a good reason for betting so strongly then it was well concealed.

'Ten pounds,' said Doug.

'Call ten pounds, and raise another fifteen,' said Simon.

Doug stopped suddenly. Nick could see that he'd been stung by Simon's bid, and that it was only now that he'd realised quite what he'd got himself into. Doug hated losing, and he especially hated losing to Simon, but that was what was going to happen. Doug didn't have the cards and Simon knew it – Christ, even *he* knew it.

'Have it,' said Doug. He took a large swig of his beer, as he tended to do if he'd just lost a hand. Well, it was early days, but so far so good.

There was nothing opportunistic about Nick's second assault – it had been carefully rehearsed. He was well acquainted with Doug's book collection, which towered over them in the living room and which he guessed Doug must have oafishly bought wholesale through mail order. All of the shelves were crammed with identical burgundy calf-leather volumes, each spotless and with its title inscribed on the spine in italicised gold. Ranging from Homer to Joyce, it was a fairly unimaginative if comprehensive attempt at the Western canon organised, to Nick's colossal and enduring amusement, alphabetically by title. Although he had looked at them many times before, at nine o'clock, as they broke for drinks and to rearrange the seating, Nick made the point of crossing the room to examine the bookshelves with exaggerated interest, tugging a too tightly wedged volume from the shelf and asking Doug in a loud voice whether he had enjoyed the new translation of Montaigne's collected essays.

It would have been a minor thing. Doug had admitted that actually he hadn't got round to reading it yet and no one, not even Simon, had smirked. But by sheer good fortune, Sophia had walked into the room seconds before. This was unusual – she was almost always out when Doug hosted poker games and if she ever was at home then she seemed to make a point of keeping out of their way. But no – she had walked through at that particular moment and, Nick could hardly believe it, she had *laughed*.

Nick taught at a secondary school, and had long mastered the taxonomy of laughter. He knew how adolescents, and therefore everyone else, laughed to hurt, befriend, bully, protect themselves, and occasionally even because something was funny. So he was well aware that Sophia had done much more than smile wryly, more even than simper. There wasn't anything giggly about it, and it certainly hadn't been a fond chuckle, he was sure about that, and anyway fond chuckles were very rare things. No, this had had a marvellous cruelty to it – it was practically a snigger, maybe even a cackle. And it had a clear direction. She wasn't laughing at what Nick had said, and let's be honest, he hadn't said anything very amusing. No, she was laughing at Doug.

Without saying anything, Sophia turned to go. Straining, Nick looked over at her across the room and for a full half-second their eyes met. There was still a smile on her face, but it was a different one now, a nice one. It was one of the most romantically charged moments that Nick had experienced in years. He already knew that Sophia read. He had noticed the books lying around the house and, unlike Doug, she did actually read them. He'd seen the paperbacks with their tea-stained covers and bent spines, and they were the same as those left around in the staff room – the better Booker prize-winners, gushing magical realism, post-imperialist genre-subverting sagas with colourful impressionist covers and endorsements by critics from the *Guardian* newspaper. The staple of book groups around the country, they were absolutely not his kind of thing at all, but that was beside the point: it was still enough for them to make a connection. It was enough for her to be, even if she didn't actually know it, *on his side*. This had proved it: for not only did she read herself, she was prepared to laugh at her husband for not reading.

Crucially, Doug had seen her laugh. It was hardly as if she'd hidden it – for whatever reason, just like Nick, she had wanted to hurt him. And, of course, she was in a much better position to do so. Doug flinched and flushed pink like Alan, but he said nothing and looked down miserably at the table, trying not to catch her eye as she walked out of the room. He had been too upset, and who knows, maybe too scared, to get cross, though that would probably follow. Hugely encouraged, Nick decided to push on with his plan. For the time being, it was clear that all the momentum and luck was with him.

For the next hour, Nick directed the conversation with intelligence and verve. This wasn't the norm. Mostly, they just bet and talked about poker hands, and if they ever did talk about anything else then it was normally Doug who led, and the discussion was confined to the everyday preoccupations of Reading's professional classes. But tonight was different. Nick had carefully prepared some topics that were intended to be of interest to everyone round the table except for Doug. He had even thought of something for Simon – a cleverly designed question as to whether a computer could ever beat a human at poker. This naturally played to Alan as well and even Vijay had something to contribute – after all, he *was* a fucking computer. Simon had bitten and a lengthy and stimulating discussion followed. It had even been enjoyable, and all the more so because Doug had been silent and grumpy for its entirety.

* * *

'Five pounds,' said Nick.

'Fold,' said Alan.

'OK, buster. Your five pounds, and I'll raise you another ten,' said Doug.

'Fold,' said Simon.

Vijay looked at Doug uneasily. His specialism was money and making quantitative assessments about companies and assets, not people. But something was going on this evening, even he knew that. What Vijay didn't know was *what* was going on. Nick was playing oddly, well, that was pretty much standard, but tonight Doug was behaving strangely as well. He had been fine to begin with, but now he seemed irritable and anxious and bad-tempered and what was he doing betting like this for? The problem was, Vijay was actually sitting on a very good hand. They had had the flop and on the table now was the four of diamonds, the queen of hearts and the ten of spades. Nothing remarkable, but he was holding the four of spades and queen of clubs, so he had two pairs already, and with still two more cards to come. This was good, he should be feeling happy with things, except that the betting was too high at this stage, and he wasn't sure why. He had long ago stopped trying to fathom Nick, but why was Doug betting like this? Did he have something powerful hidden there, maybe a pair of tens to match the one on the table, or else a jack and something else to make the straight? Or was something else going on? For some reason, Vijay suspected that, if Nick wasn't still in, then Doug wouldn't have raised like this.

'Call fifteen pounds,' said Vijay.

'Call,' said Nick.

Alan dealt the fourth card on to the table. It was the nine of clubs. It didn't do him any good, but, if one of the others was trying to build a straight, then it might help. But that depended on them playing this game properly.

'Check,' said Nick.

'Check,' said Doug.

'Five pounds,' said Vijay. If they were looking to build up winning hands, then he had to do something about it, he had to keep the betting brisk and positive, to discourage the others from going any further. That's what any good player would do now.

'Call five pounds,' said Nick.

'Your five and raise another five,' said Doug.

He said it immediately, without pausing for the slightest second. What's more, as he said it, Doug was staring fixedly into Nick's face. It was unbelievable! He hadn't given it the slightest thought! His bet bore no relation at all to the cards. Of course, if people were playing suboptimally for whatever reason, then that was all to Vijay's advantage, but it offended his sense of how things should be done. And how could he reasonably be expected to calculate what to do next? Yes, people were supposed to bluff and deceive in poker, he could hardly object to that, but they had to do it *rationally*.

'OK, call five pounds,' said Vijay. He had wanted more time to think, but Simon, always impatient whether he was in a hand or not, was scowling, and besides – he wasn't sure how much further his analysis would be able to usefully go. They were now in a world of imponderables.

'Call five pounds,' said Nick.

The fifth and final card came down. It was the five of hearts. Well, that wasn't much good to anyone, but he was still worried about the straight. The nine, ten and queen were all showing, and so there was at least a one in three chance that one of those two had got the jack. And if they did have the jack, well then there was almost a twenty per cent chance that they also had the king or the eight they needed for a straight. And what about three of a kind, that was still a possibility too.

But then if either of them really had those hands, why were they betting like this?

'Bet five pounds,' said Nick.

'I'll see that,' said Doug.

'Yes, I'll call that too,' said Vijay. He didn't know what else to do.

Like naughty schoolboys caught stealing in his father's shop, Nick and Doug turned over their cards. They had nothing! Well, not quite nothing. Doug had a pair of fours, and Nick ... no, Nick really did have nothing – not even a pair. Vijay had won. There was a bemused silence. He looked across at Simon, who shrugged his shoulders. He should be pleased – it had been a good-sized pot, but really – the whole thing was very unsatisfactory.

Nick looked over the table. Things were going very well. Doug was losing heavily and he was getting more and more agitated – more so than Nick had even hoped. There were only two main problems that Nick could see. First of all, he was losing as well and secondly he was, even more than usual, behaving like an atrocious wanker. The idea was to destroy a monster, not to become one, although Nick was sufficiently familiar with Western literature to know that this was an all too frequent consequence with these kinds of projects. Generally, it wasn't a pretty sight and involved a fair amount of misery and madness for all concerned – was he turning into Hamlet, Victor Frankenstein, Captain Ahab? Was he losing his judgement?

Well, it wasn't the time to be worrying about that just yet. He had a job to do. It was the ten o'clock break, and it was now that Nick decided to play his joker. Or as Doug would say, he went *up a gear*, he *raised the temperature* and *went for the jugular*. The others were cutting the cards for new seats, drinking bottles of beer and warily trying to assess how well everyone was doing, when Nick artfully reminded them that it was only halfway through the night and one should always bear in mind the words of the ancient Greek poet who had, so wisely, said: *Call no man happy before he dies, he is at best but fortunate.*

Nick had got away from the card table to look around all of their homes at one time or another, and Doug's study had always held a particular fascination for him. He'd had a few goes at it, and so was familiar with the idiotic quotes on the walls and the books on how to play better poker. But it was only the last time that he'd hit the jackpot and found the key sitting stupidly in the lock of Doug's desk drawer. And no wonder it was usually locked – for there inside was not only the plaque with this, admittedly quite good, quotation but also his collection of pornographic magazines. And now Doug knew that he knew. Just to make sure, Nick and he exchanged a long meaningful glance, until Doug gave in and dropped his gaze. Yes, he knew all right.

Pornography was one of the few vices that Nick had never really tried to get into – as a young man, he had found it more frightening than exciting, and now he had turned forty it just made him feel sad. So he hadn't known what to make of Doug's magazines, other than that they were obviously secret and shameful. On the basis of a quick scan, what did strike him as odd was how unattractive and out of shape so many of the women were, and how curiously ordinary. Models were supposed to be photographed reclining over chaises longues in Park Lane apartments, but this lot looked like they all lived in semi-detached houses in Hull. Did Doug have some kind of fetish or specialist sexual interest? If so, it seemed to Nick that it would only make it even more shameful. Did it have something to do with working in gyms, or was it a class thing? Maybe Doug found lower-class women arousing, in the same way that Nick had always had a thing about the upper classes, particularly if they behaved horribly towards him.

Well, whatever. The main thing was that he had possessed a weapon, and had used it to great effect. That was immediately apparent. They started up again and Doug was now all over the place – *on the ropes*, as he'd have put it. He was, Nick could appreciate, in something of a bind. He couldn't accuse him of anything because that would be self-incriminating, he couldn't just punch him because he lived on the nicest street in Reading and they were meant to be friends, and he couldn't just forget about it, because he was Doug and had just been humiliated. All he could do was try to thrash him at cards – but Nick had played enough poker now to know that that could only lead to ruin.

Vijay dealt the flop on to the table: the eight of diamonds, the jack of spades, the four of hearts. For the last thirty minutes, ever since Nick had uttered his magic words, Doug had lost nearly a hundred pounds and, other than making a series of unsuccessful and costly bets, he had barely said a thing. He hadn't moved either. Like a lump of plutonium, he sat immobile, silently radiating malice in all directions. Had Nick won this? It was too early to say just yet, but he had badly hurt him, that was clear. Nick had the seven of spades and the four of diamonds. A pair of fours. Well, that had to be worth staying in for, if only because it meant Doug was likely to do something stupid.

'Three pounds,' said Simon.

'Call,' said Alan.

'Call,' said Nick.

'Call,' said Doug.

'Fold,' said Vijay.

Vijay dealt the fourth card – the six of diamonds. Well, that wasn't much good and, by the looks of things, it wasn't going to help anyone else either.

'Three pounds,' said Simon.

'Call,' said Alan.

'Call three pounds,' said Nick.

'Call the three, and raise another ten pounds,' said Doug.

Up until now, Doug had been betting as tamely as everyone else, and he was either making such an aggressive bet now because he'd suddenly got a good hand or else, and more likely, he was *feeling* aggressive. But this wasn't going to work, Nick could see that. His betting didn't add up, nobody believed he had the hand, and besides Simon and Vijay were at the table. They weren't going to be frightened by Doug's antics – Vijay would do his calculations come what may, and all Simon would do was profit from them. As for Nick, well, he was getting out.

'Call the thirteen,' said Simon.

'Fold,' said Alan.

'Not for me,' said Nick.

Vijay dealt the final card. It was the six of clubs, a nothing card, nothing that Doug wanted anyway. Nick knew that – he was watching Doug closely. He could see the frustration and anger spread across his face. And Simon could see it too.

'I bet twenty pounds,' said Simon.

'Well, I guess it's yours then,' said Doug, with something close to a snarl, but it wasn't Simon he was angry with. It wasn't even Nick. It was *all* of them, Nick could see that.

Scratch a berk, and you'll find a wanker and, like most people who normally win things, Doug was an appalling loser. The only surprise was how quickly it had happened. In little more than an hour, his trademark big-hearted hospitality had vanished. The rubbish jokes and silly accents, the gentle self-deprecation, the shoulder-squeezing and overfriendly handshakes, the sombre congratulations whenever someone won a good hand and the stern encouragement to those who had lost – all of this had gone. His patience with Vijay had also gone. He now drummed his fingers between bets, and lavishly rolled his eyes whenever Vijay embarked on one of his mathematical journeys. In short, he had become quite as unpleasant as Nick had always hoped he was.

He was also, and Nick was really thrilled to see this, taking it out on Alan. Well, what more evidence did he need that he was doing the right thing? Nick felt himself filling up with justified indignation, one of his favourite feelings, as Doug started harassing and bullying poor Alan. The problem, and Nick did have some sympathy with Doug here, was that Alan was actually doing pretty well this evening, and had won two big hands at both of their expense. But it wasn't Nick who was getting cross about it – it was Doug who was scowling and glaring at Alan, and muttering mysterious insults under his breath and making him nervous, and who snapped at him so inappropriately and nastily when he misdealt the cards.

It was at eleven o'clock, the break before the final hour, that Doug retaliated at long last, and launched his counter-attack. And to be fair, Nick hadn't seen it coming. He hadn't been prepared for the sheer ferocity and violence of the response. Not that Doug did anything particularly clever, but there again he wasn't especially clever. Just like his gyms, what he'd always been good at was doing the simple things, even the stupid things, really well. And what he did was really quite astonishingly stupid.

Nick and Alan had been standing in the hallway, both of them unusually upbeat for this time of the night. Alan was happy because he had won so much money, and Nick because Doug had lost so much, and because he was drunk and looking at the painting again. They were drinking bottles of beer, talking about their jobs and behaving like adults. And it was at this moment that Doug came abruptly out of the nearby bathroom, and barged through them with his cock hanging out of his trousers.

Nick had almost fallen to the floor with surprise and terror. He was stunned, winded – as if he had been punched in the throat. He was paralysed, stricken with horror, unable to believe what he'd seen. As for Alan, he'd practically *fainted*. But it wasn't over yet, for now, standing in the living room, turning round to look straight into their faces, Doug gave an exaggerated apology for having bumped into them, and zipped his trousers back up, with no attempt to acknowledge this other omission. Then he had sat back down at the table, trying studiously and actually quite successfully to look as if nothing in the slightest bit unusual had happened.

Despite all those years of studying literary theory, Nick wasn't sure how usefully he could bring any semiotic analysis to bear on what had just occurred. What he did know was that, in a profound way, Doug had made his point and it had been a devastating experience. Fascinating, possibly even pornographic, but obviously without the slightest trace of eroticism. Nick felt damaged, the victim of what felt like a crude physical assault. The sheer brainless violence of it was devastating. Needless to say, Doug's penis had been simply fucking colossal. More like another arm really, a great long thick thing that swung menacingly against his trouser leg. Had he done something to pump it up? Nick wouldn't put it past him, the cheating fucker, but no – he probably hadn't even needed to. That was what being tall and good at rugby and Scottish and going to a public school gave you.

Other than Alan, there had been no other witnesses – Simon had been outside having a cigarette, Vijay had still been at the table preoccupied with counting his chips. And there was no higher authority to petition. What could he do? Nick could hardly complain that he had been intimidated by Doug's cock. It wasn't as if Doug had touched him with it or anything. And besides, they were in Doug's house, on the nicest street in Reading. What was he going to do – storm out? Call the police? Punch him?

Shaken, and also tremendously depressed, Nick and Alan returned to the table, and immediately started to lose heavily. Poker was a game for grown-ups and maybe, despite what they'd thought, they weren't grown-ups after all. They were kids, and it was Doug who was the grown-up – you only had to look at his knob to see that. If anything, it seemed to have affected Alan the worst. Alan was fucked and had collapsed into himself – he looked utterly crushed. It had been Nick's job to look after him, and he hadn't been able to. In fact, to his immense disappointment, all he could do was be spiteful to him.

Doug, meanwhile, was completely rejuvenated. So irrepressible were his spirits, flair and skill that even the others were letting him down – Simon had faded and seemed to have lost interest, and Vijay kept getting his sums wrong. In hand after hand, all dropped their cards before him or else expensively and fruitlessly plugged on to the end before folding, and when he was called, his hands were always good – his luck had come flooding back along with everything else. And, of course, he was once again being a magnificent host. The shoulder-squeezing had returned, he made stupid jokes, talked about stock-market indexes and brought in a trayful of brandies for them. And now it was Doug who was looking out for Alan, gently encouraging and consoling him when a round didn't go his way.

It was almost twelve – the last hand of the night. In a few minutes they would be reporting their performances for

Vijay's spreadsheet, and Doug would be almost certain to say it had been *a game of two halves*. Well, it had been for him at least. Nick had been losing all night, but looking across the table it seemed that Doug was back where he'd started. Alan was still, just about, up and the others were doing OK. But maybe all of that could still change because Simon had just dealt the cards and Nick had the ten and the nine of clubs.

'Two pounds,' said Vijay.

'Call,' said Alan.

'Sounds good,' said Doug.

'Call,' said Nick.

'Fold,' said Simon.

Simon dealt the flop on to the table. The three of hearts, the ten of hearts and the six of spades. So the club flush was blown and the straight looked unlikely, but at least he had a pair of tens. A pair of tens – now what could he do with that?

'Three pounds,' said Vijay.

'Call,' said Alan.

'Aye, I'll call the three, and I think we better raise it another wee bit,' said Doug, giving his squeaky impersonation of a homosexual Scottish Highlander as he threw in another two pounds. Well, that was to be expected. Doug was in the mood for raising, and another two was manageable, but the appearance of one of Doug's comedy accents was a very bad sign.

'Call five,' said Nick.

'Call,' said Vijay.

'Call,' said Alan.

Simon dealt the fourth card. It was the nine of hearts, which meant Nick now had two pairs – tens and nines. Well, that wasn't bad at all, but he never really knew what to do with two pairs. Was it a good hand or not? It was hands like this that tended to be the expensive ones, but it was also hands like this that seemed to make Simon so much of his money. Of course, he might pick up another nine or ten with the last card and turn it into a full house, but he wasn't going to count on that and, in the meantime, he was much more worried about all those hearts on the table. Did Doug have a couple of hearts in the hand – was that why he was raising so much? Or was it just because he was a big-dicked fucker?

'Two pounds,' said Vijay.

'Call,' said Alan.

'Come on! It's the last hand, so we need to liven it up a bit,' said Doug. 'Raise five pounds.' God, he was insufferable.

'Call seven pounds,' said Nick.

'Fold,' said Vijay.

'Fold,' said Alan.

Simon dealt the final card. It was the ace of diamonds. So all he'd have to play with was the two pairs, and he didn't like the look of that ace at all. The way Doug was betting, the way his luck was going, there was every chance that he had another ace. It would be just like him to have a stronger two pairs. Either that or he did have the heart flush. That was exactly the sort of thing that happened when you had this kind of hand.

There was a long pause while Doug swivelled carefully in his chair in order to look directly into Nick's face.

'The thing about poker,' said Doug slowly, 'is that it's not about how big your cock is. It's about how big you *think* it is. I bet fifty pounds.'

The fucker. The utter fucking fucker. Christ, if only Nick could hit him. If only he had the physical and mental strength to knock that bastard out cold. Now what was he going to do? He couldn't just let Doug walk away with the pot like this. Not after what that sod had done to him tonight. It was unthinkable that he folded now. Or was it? Could he really fold? Of course he was fucking going to. He had to. He had to because he couldn't afford to lose the money, because his hand wasn't good enough and his dick wasn't big enough, and because he only had two lousy pairs.

'Take it,' said Nick, and then bravely, before anyone could say anything else, he said, 'Very well played.'

Doug reached out with his arms and slowly pulled the pot towards him, grinning.

'You should have called me,' he whispered, but still loud enough for them all to hear. 'I had nothing better than a pair of sixes.'

Nick walked all the way home that evening. It was two days before midsummer and he was in need of an existentialist walk through the town at night, to remind himself that this was his life story – he was the hero, or at the very least the anti-hero, and he wasn't just a character in somebody else's. Also, it was one of his ambitions never to get banned for drink-driving again. He had a lot to think about. Clearly in some important ways he had underestimated Doug. It turned out that he wasn't a sportsman after all, and he had shown himself to be a far greater brute than even Nick had imagined. Or was he? Perhaps what he'd shown was that he was a sensitive fellow human, someone capable of being hurt by a friend, and who knew exactly how best to defend himself and to hurt back.

In truth, despite all these months of sitting round the poker table with him, Nick still didn't know his enemy. Yes, he knew that Doug was rich and right wing and had a big penis, that he had gone to a public school but had cash-economy manners, and was a bad loser and an unbearable winner, but there was so much else he didn't know. Did Doug grind his teeth in his sleep? Did he cry sometimes, for no reason, when no one else was around? Was he worried about dying? Were his dreams happy? Did he trust his wife? Did he ever wake up at four in the morning overcome with dread? On wet Sunday afternoons in November did he stare out of the window, and wonder what it was that he was meant to be doing?

Not that any of this was going to stop Nick from trying to fuck him, but wasn't it strange and sad that you could never know another person? Everyone dies alone, but did Nick have to go through all of this on his own as well? It wasn't just Doug. Simon was a mystery, a perfectly friendly but sinister blank, and all he could say about Vijay with any confidence was that he was good at adding up. And Alan? What made Alan so fearful? Nick didn't know, but he suddenly wished very much that he did. And what about their wives and children and families – what were they like? Most importantly, he very much wanted to know what Sophia was like. God, it was such a strain, so *tiring*, so heartbreakingly sad, all this not knowing.

It was one o'clock in the morning. Nick stopped to hear the solitary bell of a church that he couldn't see, and looked up at the gentle summer-night sky, smudged and smothered by the city lights. There were many other things he didn't know. Why were neon lights pink and sodium lights yellow? And the stars, the few he could see, were they always in the same place? Which constellations were which? Which ones were the planets, and how could you tell the difference?

Even the things he did know – he couldn't say *how* he knew them. The earth turned on its axis each day and it took a year to revolve around the sun, but how come he was so sure about it? Someone, a teacher, must have told him once, but how did he know it was true? Teachers were the last people to know anything. And what did the sun revolve around? Did everything revolve around something? And if so, what was it?

He crossed the Broadway. Never mind the solar system or the rest of the planet, Reading, too, was a mystery to him, though he'd lived here now for ten years. He didn't understand its buses with their non-sequential numbers and improbable routes through pernicious one-way systems. He didn't understand Reading's economy, with its defunct factories, closed-down breweries, the empty warehouses along the railway line, and its award-winning shopping centres, its bustling plaza cafés and gleaming health clubs and hotels. Maybe the answer lay in the sudden appearance of all the science parks? But then they were enigmas as well, those innocuous-looking pale-brick buildings, surrounded by well-clipped box hedges and guarded by men with dark glasses, where biotechnologists invented genetic monstrosities and cures for diseases that hadn't been discovered yet. He didn't know any of Reading's history – the gloomy churches whose bells still chimed but were lost now in the cityscape, as everything around them grew bigger and brighter, the statues in Eldon Park of the generals who fought wars that no one knew who won, and of writers who wrote poems that no one read. And he didn't know anything about his neighbours either, all those low-priority, back-of-the-queue people on Milton Road – punters and housewives, high-street shoppers and Formula One enthusiasts, with black-and-white cats and Alsatian dogs, all unhappy in ways they would never understand.

What was he sure about? He knew that it was 21 June 2009. That across the world companies merged and acquired one another, that aeroplanes crossed the skies, satellites were launched into space, and people got old and sick, and worried about bad things happening to them. He knew that every day ten thousand Africans killed one another in civil wars he'd never be interested in, that in a million human bodies a group of soft-tissue cells coalesced into a tumour, and that a hundred million *Love yous* were whispered into mobile phones and bounced back and forth from network to network and continent to continent, but that it didn't mean anything. When there was so much love, when there were so many people, then how could it?

And he knew that everyone and everything on the planet had once been stardust and would be again one day, a billion billion smithereens dispersed endlessly and helplessly across the silent universe. In the meantime, before any of that happened, he knew that the earth was round and wet and crowded and that, at the most, he had no more than fifty years left here, and he knew that people should be kind, they should try to help one another get through this, but that for some reason he couldn't, he wasn't able to, and he wouldn't. He wasn't sure why not, but he did think that it must have something to do with all his bad luck.

Round at Nick's – July

It had taken him a while, but he had finally realised that he had got the drugs thing all wrong. Or at least the wrong way round. It seemed that the general truth was that drugs fucked you up. There was no use in Nick taking cocaine or opium or heroin or whatever in order to win at cards, but there *was* the promise of significant rewards if he could get the others, specifically Doug, on to them.

Of course, Doug was never going to take them through choice. He wasn't that stupid and anyway, what with his sports centres and kids and in-laws, he was probably the type who drank heavily and happily, but had strong views on illegal drugs. No, if this was going to work, then it would all have to be done without Doug ever knowing.

Despite the practical challenges, Nick had few qualms about the enterprise. OK, he would have to acknowledge that if one of the others had spiked him with illegal and possibly dangerous drugs simply in order to beat him at cards then he would probably have gone ape-shit, but that wasn't necessarily a reason for him not to do it to them. Doug should have thought of it first. And if one really considered it, it wasn't as if what he was doing didn't have some noble and significant precedents. Duplicity, secrecy, guile – these could all be admirable qualities too. Weren't all the great heroes renowned for their cunning as much as for their courage? Not having studied any history or geography since he was sixteen, Nick only had one knowledge source to draw on, and that was Western literature. But surely that was enough? There were the audacious schemes of the Scarlet Pimpernel, the tricks of Brer Rabbit, the mischievous games of Puck, and, of course, Odysseus himself – the first and greatest hero of them all. He hadn't been a mighty warrior like Ajax or Achilles; he had been wily, a trickster. He had beaten the Trojans with a gift and defeated the Cyclops by getting him drunk first – well, that wasn't so very different from what Nick was doing to Doug now. Besides, it was sort of fair in a way, given that Nick had been so pissed himself for the last few months.

That had changed now. Now he did nothing but carefully sip his bottle of beer. His experiments with getting drunk had been illuminating but ultimately unsuccessful and probably, he now accepted, a little ill-conceived. He took another mouthful, but only because he was nervous. It was just gone eight o'clock, this was only the third hand of the evening, and he needed to play things very carefully. A lot of thought and hard work had gone into this, but the potential for a catastrophic fuck-up was still enormous.

'Raise three pounds,' said Doug.

'Call,' said Nick.

But he wasn't thinking about his hand. He was looking at Doug. How was he feeling? Was this really going to work? Doug was drinking red wine – that was a good sign. For this to go as he wanted, Doug would need to be reasonably well gone even before he was full of drugs. Christ – was this *really* such a good idea? For the last week he had veered many times between congratulating himself on his extraordinary brilliance and scrapping the whole project on the grounds that it was probably the stupidest thing he'd ever done in his life.

'Call three pounds,' said Simon.

'Call,' said Alan.

'Fold,' said Vijay.

There were now four cards on the table. Nick looked at them almost for the first time. Of course, even if it worked, there was still the problem that Doug would wake up the next morning and suspect that he had been done over. A lot depended on how drunk Doug got anyway, and on him knowing even less about drugs than Nick himself had a month ago.

It had taken a great deal of research to get to this point. To begin with, there was a bewildering number of illegal drugs to choose from and, obviously, it wasn't as if he could just ask the chemist. Though in fact that was pretty much what he ended up doing – Tim, the new chemistry teacher at school, had turned out to be exactly the kind of expert he was looking for. Nick had been careful not to go into too many details and had prepared an overelaborate cover story to explain his interest, but it hadn't been necessary – Tim had been helpfully informative and charmingly unsuspicious on the subject of psychoactive drugs.

Happily, it seemed that the kind of thing that Nick was looking for – a substance that could be easily slipped into someone's food or drink and which would dramatically fuck them up so that they behaved incredibly recklessly but wouldn't actually kill them – was widely available. It was called MDMA or, and Nick had to take Tim on trust here, methylenedioxymethamphetamine – a semi-synthetic phenethylamine thought to temporarily inhibit the uptake and breakdown of the serotonin neurotransmitter. Nick was on much firmer ground when Tim had gone on to tell him that MDMA was a soluble crystalline powder that formed the active ingredient in ecstasy.

Even Nick had heard of ecstasy, and his supplementary inter-net research soon confirmed that this was exactly what he was after. The symptoms from a standard dose included euphoria, loss of judgement, reduced risk aversion, diminished sensory awareness, mild hallucinations, impaired analytical reasoning and strong feelings of trust, affection and intimacy. In short, Doug's mind would be so profoundly and happily disorgan-ised that he wouldn't even know that he was losing a fortune at cards.

'Five pounds,' repeated Simon.

Nick looked up with a start. He had completely forgotten what he was doing. Never mind spiking Doug for now, he had a hand to play, and it was vital that he played it as casually and calmly as possible. Doug might not know anything about drugs, but he was a businessman and, Nick had to concede this, he had a shrewdness about him. If he thought that Nick was behaving oddly, playing wildly or strangely, then he might start to suspect that something was up.

'Call,' he said hurriedly.

'Fold,' said Alan.

'Yep. I'm in for five,' said Doug.

The fifth and final card came down and, to his immense surprise, Nick noticed that he had a straight. In fact, he now realised that he'd had one since the card before. It was well disguised, though that was hardly an excuse for him not know-ing: on the table there was a seven of hearts, nine of spades and jack of hearts, and there he was with the eight and ten of diamonds in his hand.

'Fifteen pounds,' said Doug.

Simon folded. For a moment, Nick wondered if he should fold as well, even though he had almost certainly got the best hand. It would have been much more in keeping with his betting, and would mean that he didn't attract anyone's attention. But no – he couldn't resist this. It wasn't often that he got to win a hand as easily as this.

'Call fifteen pounds and raise another ten,' said Nick.

'All right, I'm happy to see you for ten,' said Doug.

Nick hadn't even got round to thinking about what Doug had, and it wasn't bad at all – three jacks, but Nick's straight was a comfortable winner, and he saw now, again noticing something that had been right in front of him, that it was really quite a big pot, the biggest so far. Well, this was all very encouraging. Doug was grimacing and refilling his wine glass, and that was another good sign. Maybe this was going to work out after all.

Of course, identifying what he needed was only the start. Although every crummy little market town in the South of England was probably saturated with the stuff, getting your hands on some of this MDMA wasn't straightforward if you were a forty-year-old teacher who didn't know any drug dealers and still referred to cannabis as wacky backy. It was another teacher who came to his help – not really a surprise, as just about the only people he knew were teachers. Paul was a teacher trainee who Nick had made friends with at the beginning of the year. It was something he'd been doing for a while now – mistrusted by the more senior members of the department, Nick took it upon himself every term to be over-generous and welcoming with the new starters and trainees, which in practice meant not much more than getting them drunk, in an attempt to build up a little coterie of acolytes and impressionable allies. The strategy hadn't been as successful as he'd hoped – everyone Nick had befriended had either left under a cloud or failed to make any career progress, but it did at least mean that he knew some younger people – the kind of people who still smoked cigarettes, and drank after work, and who knew about MDMA.

Paul hadn't actually ever mentioned drugs before, but the fact that his hair was so long and curly, that he had a silver ring in his ear, like a Gypsy, and that he wore a dirty leather jacket with obscure badges on the lapels all gave Nick grounds for hope and, sure enough, after taking him for drinks and discreetly raising the subject, it soon became clear that he'd found the right guy. In fact, ever since, it had been difficult to get him to talk about anything else. Paul not only knew about MDMA but was an enthusiastic advocate and user of all recreational drugs, it was sort of his hobby, and it seemed that he'd spent most of the summer term off his head on one thing or another. Well, Nick was hardly going to disapprove of him for that and, anyway, the department head had already decided that they wouldn't be taking him on for the next year. Nick had hesitated at first to tell him exactly why he needed the MDMA, but he needn't have worried, for Paul not only approved, he had eagerly reassured him that it was a brilliant idea.

Despite all this, buying the drugs themselves had been the almost total debacle that Nick had braced himself for. His intentions were clearly good, but there was something about Paul that didn't inspire confidence and, for all his friendly assurances, he had been oddly reticent, even a bit evasive, about how and where he would get the drugs from. So it hadn't been altogether too much of a surprise when his dealer had turned out to be one of his GCSE pupils. In what he would have to consider as something of a professional low point, Nick had found himself waiting in his car one afternoon after school, keeping a lookout in case Michael Richards's mum came back home early, while Paul had been inside buying, and no doubt testing, the stuff. It was hardly ideal, but he was running out of time and anyway – the way he saw it, it was Paul who was buying drugs from a minor, not him, and it would be Paul's neck on the line if this all went tits up, not his.

It was now ten o'clock, and they would be finished in two hours. If he was going to do this, it would have to be now. The odd thing was, so far Nick was actually having the best evening he'd had for months. After his big win with the straight, he had decided to keep out of everyone's notice as much as possible. He folded early on in hand after hand if Doug or anyone else was betting heavily, he resisted any temptation to bluff and he only stayed in if he had something strong, rather than simply promising. The result of all this was that he'd lost little of his early gain, and even managed to increase it a bit, winning two or three smaller pots. He was up probably fifty pounds or so. Doug was probably down about the same, and pretty drunk by the looks of things. Alan was doing OK again, Vijay was probably down a bit, but no one, it seemed, had been doing especially well or badly. Well, that was about to change.

Preparation was everything, with something like this and Nick had spent some time designing this, crucial, part of the plan. They always broke at ten, to open a new pack of cards and change the seating arrangements. At this point, the host, unless it was Simon, usually suggested some drinks. The key thing was to make absolutely sure that Doug didn't refuse. In fact, really, to minimise any suspicion, they all needed to have one.

Trying to sound as casual as possible, Nick offered them all a drink. And then, before anyone could reply, and just in case there were any waverers, he embarked on a somewhat over-engineered explanation that today was the fifth anniversary of his mother's death, and that he always marked the occasion with a toast and a dram of her favourite whisky. Like all the most plausible stories, it had elements of truth to it: his mother was dead after all, though she had actually been a teetotaller. Anyway, it had worked like a dream – everyone had warmly accepted and said they would be delighted to honour his mother.

Before anyone could change their mind, Nick scuttled away to the kitchen to prepare the drinks. One of the many dangers with the plan, of course, was that Doug would immediately taste the MDMA and refuse to drink it, but Nick had come up with an ingenious ruse. This time he hadn't needed advice from anyone – he might not know about drugs, but spirits were another matter. He had gone to his favourite specialist off-licence and, after careful consideration, had chosen a bottle of McGuskett, an Argyll whisky familiar to people who knew about these things for its overpowering pungency and strong peaty after-taste. It was monstrously expensive and essentially undrinkable, unless one gulped it down. In fact, unless you were intending to poison someone, Nick couldn't think of any occasion when one would normally want to drink it.

The whisky was ready in the kitchen, along with five shot glasses on a tray, and, hidden underneath a biscuit tin, the sachet of MDMA, looking as if it was nothing more sinister than washing power. In fact, it had crossed Nick's mind more than once that that was exactly what it was. Having observed young Michael Richards with heightened interest over the last couple of weeks, it wouldn't be out of character, and getting conned by a sixteen-year-old in his first ever drugs deal was the kind of squalid little misfortune that Nick had come to expect over the years.

Well, there wasn't time to worry about it now. Whatever the powder was, it was vital that what happened next was done as quickly as possible. He poured the drinks, taking particular care to ensure they all had large and equal amounts, and then emptied approximately half the contents of the sachet into the glass on the rightmost side of the tray. He had given a great deal of thought as to how much to use. Paul had told him just to put the whole lot in, but he no longer trusted his judgement, and a whole gram of the stuff might be dangerous. It was absolutely essential that Doug didn't die as a result of this. Even half was probably too much, but no matter now – a good stir with the teaspoon and it had happily dissolved. The whole procedure had lasted no more than sixty seconds. Nothing had been spilt, no one had seen him, the MDMA was safely back in the cupboard and he was ready to go.

It was at this point that things became tricky. One of Nick's great fears had been that he'd get the wrong victim. It was the first time he'd done this, but he had seen enough films to know that this was precisely the kind of thing that tended to happen. Doug off his head on MDMA was one thing, but Lord knows what it would do to Alan or Vijay, or himself for that matter. Doug was sitting on his right, so as long as he was given the right-hand glass, the one in front of him, it would all be fine. And it almost certainly would have been if they hadn't gone ahead and cut the cards for new seats while he had still been in the kitchen.

In some important respects, the room he returned to was fundamentally different from the one he had left. The principal problem was that Doug was no longer sitting on the right-hand side of the table, but diametrically opposite, wedged uncomfortably into the left-hand corner. Naturally Doug was complaining about this, as he had done ever since the ProPokerPlus! had first arrived. Well, if this really did work, he wouldn't be worrying about it for much longer.

Again, preparation was everything and provided he kept his head there was no need for things to become farcical. Nick carefully rotated the tray as he walked over, in what he regarded as a perfectly natural manner. He approached the table and, like a magician holding out a fan of cards, he gently prodded the drinks towards Doug, who cheerfully accepted the one closest to him. One minute later, they had all raised their glasses to Helen Williams and gulped down the whisky. It was quite as horrible as Nick had remembered but, crucially, Doug didn't pull any more of a face than the others. He was in business.

'Five pounds,' said Simon.

'Call,' said Alan.

It was Vijay's turn to bet, but Nick wasn't looking at him. He was looking, as carefully as possible, at Doug. He had been studying him intently for the last half an hour now. Paul had told him it should start to take effect after no more than twenty minutes, but he hadn't seen anything happen yet. There again, he wasn't completely sure that he knew what to be looking for.

'Fold,' said Vijay.

'I'm happy with five,' said Doug.

'Call,' said Nick, though he was struggling to remember what cards he had.

Down came the flop. The ace of diamonds, the nine of diamonds and the nine of spades. Well, that was a pretty interesting spread of cards, but right now Nick was much more concerned with what Doug was doing.

'Bet four pounds,' said Simon.

'Your four and raise another five,' said Alan.

Doug paused, but not for any particularly unusual length of time. 'Nine pounds it is then,' he said.

'Fold,' said Nick. This was no good, he couldn't concentrate on both his cards and Doug's mental state and besides, Alan seemed to betting with an unwelcome purpose. He had, Nick thought, been doing quite a lot of that this evening.

'Fold,' said Simon. He was looking annoyed with himself.

Vijay dealt the fourth card. This one was less interesting, the six of hearts, but even so, Nick could see that this wasn't going to deter Alan, who was intent on seeing it through. But what would Doug do? Were there any clues at all from the way he was playing?

'Ten pounds,' said Alan.

'Just take it,' said Doug. He pulled a face and took another gulp of wine.

He had been losing pretty much all night, but other than that there was nothing unusual about him. Perhaps this drugs experience was going to be as disappointing as all the others Nick had ever had.

It was another ten minutes before at last something did happen: Doug started to grumble that he was far too hot, and asked Nick to turn down the heating. This wasn't a completely unfounded request – Nick's boiler was one of the house's great tragedies, the most dastardly and dysfunctional of appliances. Nick had never understood how it worked, let alone what it might be a metaphor for, and most of their attempts to break into even the lower echelons of Reading's dinner-party circuit had foundered on its spitefulness – stifling, embarrassing, sweat-drenched dinner parties, or else miserable winter nights in which guests had insisted on sitting at the table in their overcoats. But tonight, as Nick knew, it was behaving itself, mainly because it was switched off. It was a late-July evening, it had rained most of the day, and the temperature in the house was comfortable, maybe even slightly cool. If Doug was overheating, then something else was at work. Tim had told him that heightened body temperature was one of the results of taking MDMA, and Paul had stressed the importance of having lots of water to drink. Well, Doug was at least still drinking plenty of wine.

Alan was dealing the cards. Doug was buying another hundred pounds of chips. It was hard to tell for sure, but there was an urgency about him now, which was more than just the impatience of someone who wanted to make good his losses. He was frenetically stacking up his new chips in front of him, rubbing his hands and muttering opaque threats and pieces of swear words. It was all starting to look promising.

It had just gone a quarter past eleven. Vijay dealt the last card – the three of diamonds. Already on the table was a six, a nine, a jack and a two.

'Raise ten pounds,' said Simon.

'Fold,' said Nick.

'Your ten and raise another twenty-five,' said Doug.

'OK, I'll see you for twenty-five,' said Simon. 'What have you got?'

To the general astonishment of the table, Doug had a pair of sixes. And in the previous hand he had bet thirty pounds on the basis that he had a queen. Things were well and truly happening. Doug was now playing incredibly bad poker. It had been observed before that after having drunk too much wine he tended to play with unwarranted confidence, but tonight he had drunk too much wine and taken a substantial quantity of a mood-enhancing drug. The result was the most expensive thirty minutes at the poker table in the group's history. In what amounted to a stunning reversal of fortune, all of Nick's previous loss-making records were being eclipsed.

It wasn't just the cards. In a variety of ways, it was now clear that Doug had gone bananas. He was rocking up and down in his chair, repeatedly chanting what sounded like *Sophia* in a low and mournful moan. His sentences had now completely fragmented, and everything he attempted to say collapsed into half-completed riddles and snatches of Scottish folk song. Although, remarkably and impressively, he would occasionally shout out what seemed to be entire sentences in Greek.

What was more, Doug also looked outrageously dreadful. Of course he had never been a good-looking man, but Nick was more than mildly fascinated, and also a little worried, by how horrible he had now become. As far as he knew, the drugs were meant to reorganise his brain, not his facial features, but this was pretty much what seemed to have happened. His forehead was bulging, the whites of his eyes had disappeared, his eyebrows had clamped themselves together, his nostrils were flared like a horse's, his mouth was doing something extraordinary and Christ on earth – what was going on with his jaw? He looked like Cro-Magnon man, a protohuman. He looked like he was capable of great acts of physical endeavour and violence, but very little else.

Alan was gaping at Doug as well, and looking thoroughly alarmed. It had occurred to Nick that this might have all gone too far, but one of the problems with these things was that there didn't seem to be any way of switching them off. He had tried to ask Paul about it, but it was another thing he had been vague about, and he had had little advice to give on the matter, other than that if by some chance Doug fell unconscious then it was important to drop him outside the hospital, and not actually go in with him. Well, thank Christ, that at least didn't seem likely to happen, not yet at any rate. Right now, Doug was the opposite of unconscious.

There was a real danger that he might start destroying the furniture. It was old and fragile and in many ways wouldn't be missed, but Nick would have to see it as an unwelcome development. There was an air of unhinged lawlessness about Doug right now that Nick was concerned about. It was vital that he controlled the situation, and that Doug remained the victim of all this, not the other way round. The others, too, were clearly getting uncomfortable. Doug was having the time of his life, but an uneasy atmosphere had settled around the rest of the table. Alan was obviously unhappy, and Vijay looked deeply troubled. Of course, Simon was more worldly and may have begun to suspect that something other than wine and whisky was responsible for all this, but Nick didn't think he would be especially interested in finding out what. The only interest that he ever really took in them was making money, and he was certainly doing that tonight.

It was now ten minutes to midnight. Doug had already announced that he wanted to play on all night, or else go out to a nightclub, but there was little support for either suggestion. They would end at twelve, as usual, which meant that Nick had just one or two hands to profit from all this. So far, it seemed that everyone was benefiting except him. Well, not everyone – Vijay with his careful calculations and percentages was doing much the same as always, and appeared to be largely oblivious to the fact that one of his opponents had gone mad. But the others, Alan and Simon, were making tremendous amounts of money.

For the last time that evening, Alan dealt the flop. The king of diamonds, the nine of spades and the ten of hearts.

'Fifteen pounds,' said Doug. 'Fifteen pounds. I'm going to bet fifteen fucking pounds, and Sophia is not going to stop me.'

OK, well, maybe this was his chance. Nick had the king of hearts and the queen of spades in his hand – so he had a pair of kings, not bad at all. Meanwhile, Doug was already betting like a lunatic.

'Fold,' said Vijay.

'Fold,' said Simon.

'Call,' said Alan.

Well, that wasn't what you'd normally expect from Alan but, for all his concerns, he had clearly twigged some time ago that Doug was throwing money away and he was determined to make the most of it.

'See your fifteen and raise another ten,' said Nick.

'See your ten and raise another ten,' said Doug.

Had he even looked at his cards yet? Nick wasn't at all sure that he had. For the last ten minutes, he had become fixated on the spotlight above the table, and was staring at it, in a curious and unblinking fashion, with the palms of his hands spread out in front of him. Although he appeared to have calmed down, this wasn't necessarily much comfort. Was he going into a trance? The sooner he got him out of the house the better.

'Fold,' said Alan.

That at least made things easier – the point of all this was for him to destroy Doug, not for Alan to exploit the situation. He wasn't even interested in beating Alan. He was doing this for *all* of them – couldn't they see that? But Nick could hardly explain it to them. He was pretty certain that, if they ever found out, the others would take an incredibly dim view of all this.

'Call,' said Nick.

Alan dealt the fourth card into the centre, and it was a big one – the king of clubs. The straight was still a possibility, but more importantly he now had three kings. By anyone's standards, that was a very good hand indeed – particularly when you were up against someone off his head on drugs.

'I'm going to bet ten pounds,' said Doug. 'And everyone else can go screw themselves. It's my money and my bet.'

'Your ten and raise another twenty,' said Nick.

Doug was animated again – whatever it was that had been absorbing him for so long suddenly didn't appear to be of any interest after all. He was looking at his cards and looking at the cards on the table with spasms of excitement. He started to rock back and forth in his chair again. He was cracking his knuckles, and clicking his fingers, and stamping his feet and making peculiar, irritating noises with his tongue against his teeth.

'Call your twenty pounds,' he said.

The final card came down. It was the nine of clubs. Now that meant he had a full house – three kings and a pair of nines. It was a spectacularly good hand, the best of the evening. Of course, in normal circumstances, he would now be frantically trying to suppress how he felt about it and to appear as underwhelmed as possible, but this evening he really didn't have to bother. Doug was completely incapable of divining anything that might be going on outside his own mind. He wasn't rocking in his chair any more – he was bouncing. He was veering dramatically up and down in his seat, he had started singing again. And now he *had* broken the chair, the idiot, and what's more barely even noticed. He was on his feet, he was clapping his hands and babbling incoherently, possibly religiously, and then, dramatically pulling himself upright, standing as tall and as still as he possibly could, he pronounced in a tone of striking solemnity, 'I'm going to bet thirty pounds.'

'Call your thirty and raise another fifty,' said Nick.

This was, he knew, leading to one of the most glorious moments of his entire life. He had half expected it to be sullied and complicated by guilt or pity at this point, but fortunately that didn't seem to be happening at all. Doug was poisoned and witless and deranged and a fellow human being, almost a *friend* really, but it didn't seem to matter right now.

Besides, Doug wasn't even giving him the time to feel differently about things. For as soon as Nick had bet, he had jumped up again and said, 'Call your fifty and raise another – oh fuck, wait, hold on a minute.'

They had hit a difficulty. Doug had managed to use up all of his remaining chips, and there was a discussion, expertly led by Vijay, as to how to resolve it. Doug was largely oblivious to the details of this, as he was pacing up and down on the other side of the room, swinging an imaginary golf club and talking about Arnold Palmer. Since Doug was out of chips and it was the last hand of the night, the issue was whether Nick was prepared to let his bet stand, or else insist that Doug be able to bet no more than what he had in front of him. Showing just the right amount of equanimity and dignity, Nick quietly agreed to the request and to accept the bet in full.

At long last they were back round the table. Doug had been persuaded to sit down, but now Vijay had risen to his feet, watching in spellbound horror and excitement. There was almost four hundred pounds' worth of chips in the centre. Alan couldn't bear to look. Simon was shaking his head, doubtless wishing that he had had a hand worth staying in for.

Only Nick remained calm. His moment had arrived. All the intelligent, careful work of the last few weeks was at last coming to fruition. Yes, he'd had some help, and he would make sure to reward Paul and Tim, and even Michael Richards could look forward to some very good marks in his essays next term, but their roles had been essentially incidental. It had been his vision and this would be his victory. Slowly, making sure that the others could all share and appreciate what he'd done for them, he revealed his cards to a chorus of sighs and nods of the head. A full house – one of the very greatest hands in poker. Vijay gave a little clap of the hands, and Simon wasn't shaking his head any more, he was gently nodding with respect. It was a hand worthy of a four-hundred-pound pot. And now it was Doug's turn. Poor Doug – he really was a ghastly mess. Not even his cock could save him now. His hands were trembling and his head was juddering, and he was whispering elaborate incantations under his breath as if he believed that somehow his cards could be changed by magic. It was quite possible that he still had no idea what they were. But his doom could be delayed no longer, and Doug now turned over his cards. Even this was now almost beyond him – he fumbled and pawed, and he looked up at them all with a heartbreakingly childlike smile. He had four nines.

Nick had only the haziest memories of what happened after that, though, judging by the complaints from the neighbours the next morning, there had probably been a great deal of howling and singing and more stamping of feet from Doug. Of course, this being poker night, he did get to hear Vijay announce the precise improbability of such a thing happening. And he did remember Doug embracing him tightly, sobbing with wonder and joy. Standing on one of the remaining chairs, he had given a long and incoherent speech to the effect that this was the happiest moment of his life, more important and profound than his wedding day or the birth of his children. To make matters worse, Doug then offered to share the pot with him, on the grounds that he loved him, and that what they had just gone through together must never damage their friendship.

Two hours later, long after they had all gone and Doug had been carried into a taxi, Nick was still sitting at the table. It was fortunate that he had written his undergraduate dissertation on absurdist drama all those years ago. It was, he supposed, the first and most important piece of preparation he'd done for the evening. It meant that he knew, of course, that no one ever laughs at the biggest jokes. It wasn't because they weren't funny, but rather because no one ever got to hear them – except dying men, or angels or God or maybe the stars. For the biggest jokes were the cosmic ones. They were the jokes that ricocheted across the universe, that echoed down through the aeons and dissolved human souls. Somehow, Nick had done that rarest of things – he had made a cosmic joke. In fact, and he had to accept the possibility now, he may even *be* one. But that didn't mean that he could laugh. For you never laughed at your own joke, no matter how big or how funny it might be. No – you didn't even smile. Instead, the likelihood was that you would just start to gently cry.

As well as being a metaphysical and moral disaster, the cost of this escapade had been simply incredible. On top of the massive loss at cards there had been the drugs themselves, the whisky, the broken furniture and all those evenings buying that fucking idiot Paul drinks in the pub. What's more, in the later stages of his frenzy, Doug had managed to spill an entire glass of red wine over his poker table, though he supposed that he could hardly blame him for that.

He poured himself another thick glass of the McGuskett. This was his third or fourth and it was actually starting to taste quite reasonable. That had to be a bad sign. Janet was away for the night visiting friends he had never heard of, and apparently had met several times. Well, that was probably just as well because he'd already decided that he was going to sleep where he was tonight. In a very important sense he was giving up – not necessarily on Project Fuck Doug, but on other things, things he hadn't even realised he still believed in until this evening. He pressed his forehead down on to the soft smooth baize of the ProPokerPlus! and, thankfully, fell asleep almost immediately. He dreamt that he was in the middle of a group of Shetland ponies, huddled together on a wind-blasted and rain-soaked moor, and that he felt warm and happy, but he would never remember it afterwards.

Round at Alan's – September

Being a teacher was like having two birthdays every year – your own, in which you became a year older, and 1 September, in which everyone else became a year younger. Since they amounted to the same thing, it was hard to say which was the more depressing, but the start of each school year had become an increasingly greater source of dread and misery. Although he had managed to keep it going for longer than he had ever expected, Nick no longer tried to rationalise what he did for a living on the standard grounds that passing knowledge down from one generation to the next was an honour, that education was the highest of endeavours and teaching the noblest of professions. No – he was a teacher because the holidays were good and because he couldn't think of a single other thing that anyone would ever pay him to do.

It didn't help that, despite having spent three years trying to get a job there, he now found the school he worked at completely disgusting. It was one of the best state schools in Berkshire, which meant that it was full of exactly the kind of cocksure little fuckers that had ruined his own adolescence. Fourteen-year-old boys who were already determined to read business studies at university and work in financial services, ambitious teenage girls who wanted to work in public relations and had a way of making you feel gauche and no good at your job. And the parents! Jesus Christ, anyone would think they were paying, the way they went on at you. Which meant, of course, that the headmaster, a massive sod, and the head of the English department and every other bastard in between were also always on at you. Thankfully, it was still a comprehensive – there were enough dolts and poor kids to even things out a bit, but Nick wished he was back teaching at one of those war zones in South Reading, at the school he'd spent years trying to get out of, where no one bothered turning up for parents' evening, and you could say what you liked in class, safe in the knowledge that none of the kids had a clue and would never amount to anything anyway.

So there should have been every reason to feel quite as unhappy and demoralised as he always did at this time of year, except that he didn't. It was partly of course because he was enjoying the economic crisis so much, but also because something quite extraordinary had happened. Something so stupendously unlikely and exciting that, even though it had happened almost a week ago, he could focus on little else.

'Nick, it's you to bet,' said Simon. 'It's five pounds.'

'Sorry, was miles away. Yes, call five pounds,' said Nick.

'Call,' said Alan.

'That's fine with me,' said Doug. 'Let's have the next card.'

Nick had been miles away, but not that many miles – only one or two at the most. For what he was thinking about, what he'd been thinking about all night, was the evening he'd spent in a nothing-special pub just at the edge of town, opposite the College of Further Education, with, of all the people in the world, and just you wait for this one, Doug . . . Sophia fuck-ing McLain.

Funnily enough, it was Janet who had got Nick into adult education. Or rather harassed and badgered him into it.

Realising that his teacher's salary alone wasn't going to get the new kitchen she wanted, she had discovered that many of his colleagues spent their Mondays after school teaching evening classes and university-access courses. He had managed to resist the idea for six months, but her persistence was unyielding and, ultimately, her question unanswerable – what *else*, apart from the internet, did he do on a Monday night?

And, of course, he had loved it as soon as he started. What a pleasure it was to be teaching people who were more frustrated and depressed than he was! But there was more to it than being able to feel superior at last – he actually liked the people he was teaching. In fact, there was even more to it than that: they seemed to like him as well. They got on. They were *his* people. The lost tribe of Nick Williams – not psychopaths or career criminals or vagrants or anyone glamorously dangerous or really fucked up, but all those people for whom, somehow, for one reason or another, it just hadn't happened. Those people with not terribly good jobs or nice houses or pretty wives, who tended to get things wrong more often than right, and who were always making bad decisions and had bad luck.

Nick wasn't political. He had long ago stopped voting for Labour or anyone else, and now he didn't even have a political outlook. True, there were lots of people and things he didn't like, but that hardly constituted a coherent world view. He didn't like rich people or Americans or public schools or contemporary art or postmodernism or the *Guardian* newspaper or London or the Conservative Party or trade unions. Sometimes he worried if he was turning into a crypto-Fascist, or maybe an anarcho-Leninist. But no, there was still *something* he believed in, something important. He believed in second chances. He believed that people, no matter how foolish or selfish or wicked they might have been, all deserved another go. It was what adult education was all about. It was what he and his people were all about. Although, and he did at least know this was odd, he also believed in the death penalty.

Financially, adult education wasn't the bonanza that Janet had being hoping for. For one thing, he quickly got into the habit of frittering away much of what he earned in the pub afterwards eating chips and drinking beer with the students, and then of course, what little money he had saved ended up going on the ProPokerPlus! anyway. But for Nick, at least, there had been other benefits, which had become apparent as soon as he'd started: the women he taught found him attractive. In a way, he shouldn't have been surprised. It was a natural thing – students fall in love with their teachers in the same way that young girls like ponies and adolescent boys fantasise about schoolfriends' mothers. It happened to Mary Shelley and Eliza Dolittle, to Plato and Sylvia Plath, and it happened on a regular basis to the bored housewives and secretaries who flocked every September to Reading College of Further Education. Nothing very interesting about that, of course, and though he had always enjoyed and cultivated the attention, he had never done anything about it. He wasn't *that* stupid. But this time, with Sophia, he might just have to be. If ever there was a time to be reckless, surely this was it? Just think what she could tell him, how good it would be to talk to her for a bit, maybe get to know her properly. There were some huge risks obviously and he'd need to be disciplined about things, but provided he was smart about it, provided he wasn't *too* fucking reckless, then no harm need come to anyone, except Doug of course.

Vijay turned over the fourth card. It was the queen of hearts. On the table already was the jack of hearts, the two of hearts and the eight of spades. Nick didn't have any hearts in his hand, and wasn't quite sure what he was still doing in this round.

'Check,' said Simon.

'Sounds good,' said Nick. 'I'll take a check as well.'

'I'll bet ten pounds,' said Alan.

'Call ten pounds,' said Doug.

'Fold,' said Simon.

Alan seemed to have been doing a lot of that sort of thing this evening, and by the look of things was up quite a bit. In fact, now that he thought about it, and heaven knows he'd tried to do everything he could to forget that evening, Alan had also done pretty well last time. There were other things about Alan that seemed different. For one thing, he wasn't wearing glasses any more. It made a big difference. Handsome would probably be pushing it, but certainly a lot less pathetic. But it was more than just the glasses. He had a way about him now that Nick had never seen before: he seemed alert rather than anxious and had a stringy kind of toughness to him, as if he was someone capable of hurting instead of just being hurt. Well, that was the last thing he needed. It was one thing to lose every single month, but quite another to be the *only* loser, particularly the one who earned the least amount of money. It just didn't seem very fair.

The question now, of course, was what he should do about it. Obviously he wasn't about to start fucking Alan, but the need for vengeance was greater than ever. The real problem, the eternal enemy, had always been Doug, and he had just been given a golden opportunity to fuck him up for good. But how best to go about it? His last attempts had hardly been an unmitigated success, and this new plan was, if not quite as stupid, then certainly as dangerous. In any case, what exactly was the plan? The thing with Sophia was nascent at best. The potential was there all right: you only had to look at how Doug's face had shuddered and twisted when he'd mentioned the classes at the start of the night. But still, a couple of drinks and the brushing of fingers as they shared a bowl of chips was hardly going to bring Doug's world to an end. If this was going to go any further, then something a lot bolder was required.

Yet did he really dare? Raising the stakes wasn't something that had ever done him much good at the card table, and nor had hanging on in, expensively hoping for the right card to come along. But there again, folding never got you anywhere either, and playing it safe didn't win you the big pots. Perhaps, for once, he should try to weigh up the odds on all of this, undertake a cost-benefit analysis: assess the dangers, what the prize was, what he wanted, what he feared. But how do you even begin? Was that really how other people did things? Nick could barely calculate the probability of drawing three of a kind, never mind working this one out.

'Nick, it's your bet. Ten pounds,' said Doug.

'Oh fuck. Yeah, sorry. Fold,' said Nick.

Doug glared over at him. Nick had been doing this all evening and it was starting to get on his nerves. Trying to work out what Nick was thinking was hard enough even when his mind was on the game, but if he was going to drift off like this then Christ knows what would happen – he might start *winning* or something.

Doug had a lot to think about tonight, and it wasn't just the fact that he had somehow got to this stage without any bloody hearts in his hand. Not so long ago, of course, that wouldn't necessarily have been a problem. He would have ridden it out, chased Alan off with a big fuck-off bet and a good hard stare, but Alan seemed to have changed. Somehow, for some reason, he'd toughened up. He didn't flinch or go pink any more, or fold his cards in panic and relief. He could hold people's gaze now, and calmly assess what call to make.

It wasn't just Alan who had changed – *he'd* changed as well. He could tell that. The fearlessness wasn't there any more.

He felt vulnerable, at risk. Even at home, locked away behind the oval doors, the pebble drive and iron gates, sitting behind his desk and reading golfing magazines, he would start to feel uneasy. It was partly that fucker Nick's fault for sniffing around in there. That had started him off, but now he couldn't help himself. He didn't feel in charge any more. Things were going on that he was no longer able to control. He was also getting outnumbered: more and more Lakises kept turning up from Cyprus and taking positions in the business. What had happened to the immigration laws in this country? He could still trust the twins and the dog, but he was getting less and less sure about the rest of his family. It was meant to have been *his* takeover all those years ago, but it didn't feel like that any more.

And what about Sophia? How did she fit into all this? She was his wife, but whose side was she really on? And how would he ever summon up the courage to ask her? He wasn't even sure that she liked him any more. Well, they'd been married eight years now, you'd expect things to change, for certain feelings to lessen and weaken. But it had always been his understanding that other feelings would then come along to take their place. Other *nice* feelings – warmth, understanding, companionship. Sophia certainly didn't seem to have any of those. She didn't take any interest in his hobbies either – not even poker. In fact, the only thing she was ever interested in was *reading*. Hence all the endless book groups and now the bloody evening class. And who ends up teaching the class? Nick, that's who, and didn't he look fucking delighted about it? No wonder Doug was starting to feel paranoid.

But just when he needed to be at his most authoritative, he could feel his strength ebbing. His father-in-law seemed more vigorous than ever, certainly more foul-tempered, but something quite different seemed to be happening to Doug. He still kept to his training programme, he still did two hours in one of his clubs every single day, but it wasn't working any more. No matter how hard he pounded the machines and threw his body against the mats, he knew he was weakening. By the end of every day he felt a little heavier, less nimble, closer to death. Also, he was sure his penis was getting smaller.

It was even worse than that – *Reading* was changing. As the years had gone by, he had found it hard to distinguish between himself and the town he had lived in for so long. He knew how the place worked just as well as he understood his own body. How well he knew and cherished its rhythms: the eight o'clock traffic jams on the ring road, the little electric bus forever going round and round the business parks, the fidgety mid-morning queues at the cash-point on Broad Street, the rotating adverts in the estate agent's windows on Caversham Road, the smell of Eldon Park after a summer rainstorm and the sound of low rumbles from the bars and pubs on Friar Street, as the night-time economy flickered into life on a Friday evening.

But something was going wrong, something that he hadn't ever seen before. There was a contingency about it all now, an insubstantiality that he had never noticed. Had none of it been real after all? He didn't know which sources he could trust. He had stopped taking the *Financial Times*, in truth he had always found it unreadable anyway, but it wasn't just that one – all of the newspapers now filled him with dread, and the television news was unwatchable. What about all those structural-finance consultants and e-business analysts and intellectual-property lawyers who had filled up his health clubs – had they all just been imagined by someone? Had their jobs all stopped being real?

It was much more than just a question of economics. He despised economics, like all of his great business heroes.

Economics was just something that people like Nick and Simon talked about, but he had to deal with more practical considerations. Doug had invested an incredible amount of money in his latest health club, easily the biggest and most technically advanced of them all – a flagship for his chain. What's more he hadn't just disagreed with the old man's advice on this one, he had ignored it. He had borrowed heavily, much more than his father-in-law knew, or Sophia for that matter. It was just as well. Had he overdone it? He was worried that he had, worried that his judgement had, at long last, failed him. The whole premise of the new club was that it was going to be really really fucking expensive. This one wasn't being built for computer programmers or accountants. It was high-concept, it was a thing of immense grace and wonder, and it was intended for all those professionals and entrepreneurs who suddenly, bewilderingly, didn't seem to exist any more.

Vijay dealt the fifth and final card – the ace of diamonds. Well, well – that changed things a bit. Not only was it, thank Christ, not another heart but also it gave him two pairs – aces and jacks, not bad at all. Very good in fact. Perhaps this was going to be his hand after all. Reading might no longer be under his control, but at least he still had it in him to rule this little table.

'Bet thirty pounds,' said Alan, almost as soon as the card was down.

Doug stared long and hard at Alan. Not only was he not backing down any more, he had turned into something of a bluffer. Of course, he used to be hilariously bad, and ever since he'd told him all those months ago that nonsense about having a tell he had started hyperventilating as soon as he bet a pound more than his hand was worth. But there was none of that now. Now Alan had an impenetrable iciness to him, almost like Simon, and without his glasses there was a hardness about the way he held himself, a don't-fuck-with-me look that he'd never had before. Christ – what should he do? He had the better hand, he was sure of it – but how sure? He wasn't certain, he wasn't totally confident about it. In fact, he wasn't sure at all. Alan had been betting strongly all the way along, as you would if you had two hearts in the hand for the flush, or, of course, if you were a presumptuous little fuck who was trying to steal the pot with a bluff.

Alan was staring back at him now, and even appeared to have the slightest of smiles on his lips. This was scarcely believable. He needed more time to think, but Alan, *Alan*, was trying to hurry him along. He took a sip from his sparkling water. That was something else that had changed, and probably not before time. Doug had had a summer off from the drink, and even now, in late September, was still cautious about restarting. The last hangover, after that night at Nick's, had been an astonishing, life-changing experience. He didn't want to go through anything like it ever again. Christ knows, he didn't think he'd had *that* much to drink, though that whisky Nick had given them had been pretty potent. All in all, it had been something of a wake-up call. He was forty-four years old. There was no point in pretending otherwise – his body couldn't take it any more. More to the point, his *mind* couldn't take it. That was the real problem. For a full week after that night, he had been in an astounding state. He'd never suffered mental illness before, in fact he'd never really believed it existed, but he was prepared to accept now that that's what had happened. Other than that, he simply wasn't prepared to think about it ever again.

Nick suddenly gave a loud and exasperated sigh. Trust him to get in on the act. As if he didn't know he had to make a call. As if it had anything to do with that fucker. Simon was fidgeting as well, of course, and looking at his watch. Well,

OK then, he'd make a fucking call. He'd give them what they wanted.

'Fold,' said Doug, and stomped off into the kitchen to find another bottle of water.

It was ten o'clock, and they had broken for drinks and snacks. Nick was in the bathroom upstairs, and was absent-mindedly searching through Alan's medicine cabinet. It was something he liked to do from time to time, and over the years he'd managed to comprehensively root around almost all of their houses. Although, apart from Doug's pornographic magazines, he'd never come across anything especially sensational. He had found Alan's sleeping pills, Vijay's hair dye and Sarita's electric hair-remover, but that was about it. Simon had been his principal interest; he had been hoping for some clues, some deep and dark secret that would unlock him, but he'd found nothing, not even any family photographs. Nothing except philosophy books, paperback thrillers and boxes of duty-free cigarettes.

Anyway, even if he didn't find anything, it was always good to get away from the others for a bit, and have some space to think. He needed to think about Doug for one thing. Doug was labouring tonight, that was obvious, and wasn't his normal unbearable self. On the face of it that ought to be a good thing, but, if Doug had a lot on his mind, then what was it? Doug was hardly likely to be worrying about the brevity and futility of human existence, but maybe the recession was getting to him? Or was it marriage problems? Well, that would fit. He'd noticed that Sophia had been careful to mention Doug as little as possible that evening, but perhaps he could get more out of her. For the hundredth time he thought back to that other night, three months ago, when she had laughed at Doug so heartlessly, so encouragingly, for not having read the right books.

Of course, he had had to introduce himself to her at the class – she hadn't recognised him at first. Not that this was really such a surprise – they had only met a handful of times, and on each occasion he had been playing poker with the others, and she had been hurrying to get somewhere else. But he had recognised her right away. Over the years of playing poker at Doug's, he must have spent many hours looking at her picture. Not that ghastly family portrait in the hall, but those silver-framed photographs that were scattered around the McLain household, each one like a splinter from a smashed mirror, reflecting back all that wealth and prestige and good luck.

Sophia had registered to do the course in modern and contemporary literary fiction. Well, that had made things easy. For once it felt like he really did have home advantage. It was an introductory evening, there was no formal teaching, and he had sat on the front desk in his jeans and leather jacket, the top buttons of his shirt undone, his legs astride, discussing reading lists and favourite authors. With the very mildest of prompts, they had all left the FE College, with its faintly buzzing overhead lights, orange plastic chairs and breeze-block walls, and moved across the road to the Rose and Crown. And now he really *was* at home. This was Nick Williams at his most glorious and best, he knew that. Like the Atlantic salmon leaping up waterfalls, and the golden eagle swooping down from the granite crags, he was at his most magnificent in the Rose and Crown, with a pint of beer and some ready-salted crisps, talking about the state of the postmodern novel.

The other students and teachers had drifted off, Nick had been talking about Samuel Beckett, but amazingly, Sophia was still there. It was scarcely believable – she was actually interested in what he was saying! No, it was much more than that, she was interested in *him*. Or was she? And *why*, for Christ's sake? A week later, and round after round of replaying it in his mind, and he still didn't know. But he had to find out. He had to. So much depended on it, even if he wasn't sure what.

It had been a Monday evening, she had had two small glasses of wine, he had had four pints of beer – clearly nothing was going to happen, and they had parted outside the pub without the slightest hesitation or charged awkwardness. But then he had done something else. In a highly daring and controversial move, which he was still in two minds about, the very next afternoon he had sent her in the post a collection of short stories by Jorge Luis Borges. Whatever the wisdom of what he'd done, it had been a cunningly chosen gift – after all, this was what he knew best – and it was the kind of book that someone like Sophia would be intrigued by, and that he could talk about at great length. He had also written a suitably charming but not in the least bit provocative ten-word inscription that had taken him two hours to compose. But now what? The classes themselves didn't start for another couple of weeks. Should he just wait until then, or would that be odd? Would it come across as gentlemanly or unfriendly? Or perhaps it was for her to make the next move: is that how it worked? He was well aware that, in a number of important ways, he didn't have a fucking clue what he was doing.

And then, just as he was about to leave, he saw them. Not in the medical cabinet after all, but he caught the little square yellow box out of the corner of his eye, on the very top shelf above the bath. Clearly Alan didn't want anyone to see it and no wonder for, after standing on a chair and inspecting further, Nick found a three-month supply of antidepressant tablets. So that was what was going on! Well, that certainly explained a few things: that's why Alan was betting with so much confidence these days, the fucking *cheat*. That was where his new-found steeliness and good luck had come from. Jesus Christ, it was getting impossible to trust anyone.

Nick carefully examined the packaging. He had heard that these things had come a long way in recent years, and didn't fuck you up like they used to. Inside the box was a folded piece of paper with a detailed description of how the tablets worked by targeting and activating, or maybe blocking and deactivating, neurotransmitters, which was all largely unintelligible but sounded vaguely familiar from his conversations in the summer with Tim the chemistry teacher. Maybe these worked like the MDMA, although a bit more manageable. The effects were clear enough, though: alleviation of anxiety, removal of phobias, lessening of engrossing and troubling thoughts. Well, you couldn't argue with that – that was pretty much what everyone he knew needed. There were some side-effects of course: increases in energy, weight loss and delayed ejaculation, but even they sounded magic.

Nick carefully put the box back. Well, that had given him something to think about, but he mustn't get distracted from the task in hand. Besides, he wasn't like Alan. He wasn't anxious all the time, he was *angry* all the time; he wasn't depressed, he was oppressed; and his problems had little to do with how he felt, he was sure of that. No, the problem wasn't his inner space, it was outer space, it was the universe and all the terrible things in it, including himself. And what would happen if he did start taking medication to sort himself out? What would be left of him once the bitterness and disappointment and rage and hurt and bad luck had all gone? What would he be then? He'd just be a fucking *loser*, that's what.

Alan didn't believe in God. He didn't believe in people either. He wasn't a humanist, he was a technologist. Western society had created this mess and Western science would have to solve it. Happily it usually did. Unlike other faiths, his belief in technology was well founded. It had, largely, sorted out his crooked teeth at the age of thirteen, the asthma and eczema that had blighted his student years, and when the insomnia and 3 a.m. panics had started in his thirties, the sleeping pills had got him through the nights. Now, once again, at the age of forty, science had come to his rescue – it was the only thing that ever had.

He had undergone a pretty comprehensive fit-out over the summer. It was long overdue. He had needed a major physical and neural overhaul, a systems upgrade and a reboot. Christ, what he had really needed was *atomic* therapy – the complete reconfiguration of as many of his molecules as he could possibly afford. If he'd had the money, of course, he would have gone to California for the full works and got himself a dick like Doug's, shored up his hairline and maybe done something about his nose but even so – there was still plenty he could do.

First of all, they had sorted out the whole reproduction problem. All those fretful and shameful months of trying to produce a baby for themselves had come to an end. They went to see a specialist in London and he was pronounced subfertile, and Alice wasn't much better either. No matter – they had accepted it calmly, and then embarked in a businesslike manner on doing something about it. In the natural world they wouldn't have a baby, but there was nothing natural about where he lived. It was the South of England in the twenty-first century, he worked in computers and nature didn't come into it. If they wanted a baby, then they'd get one. And it wasn't so bad – it would be made in a glass beaker and inserted into Alice by a team of doctors, but at least their baby was going to be *his*, at least it would inherit his genetic defects and no one else's. As far as Alan was concerned, as far as the human species was concerned, he had done what was required.

Next, he'd got his eyes lasered. This was, he admitted, something of an extravagance, but why not? He was tired of being so short-sighted, of looking so exactly like he imagined himself to look. Contact lenses had made his eyes water, and made him blink and twitch like a cartoon mole, and because of his stigmatism his spectacles had great thick goggle-eyed lenses that as a young man had made him look as if he had one of the milder learning disabilities. It was especially unfortunate, because his eyes were actually his best feature: a surprisingly strong deep blue, which suggested a depth of character that he'd never had. And, of course, if his blasted tell had been something to do with glasses, well, that solved that problem as well – though, in any case, he'd stopped worrying about that now.

Given that he'd been dismally short-sighted since he was six years old, the whole procedure had been remarkably easy. Another couple of trips to a specialist clinic in London, a cheque for five thousand pounds, and then he had sat down in a dark room one afternoon, his head and shoulders had firmly but kindly been put into a cushioned brace, and he had been subjected to some disconcerting flashes of blue light. After that he'd slept for a bit and, when he removed the bandages that evening, he could see perfectly. And that was it! Entire world religions were built on lesser miracles.

And finally, he'd got himself a prescription of antidepressants. Again, it turned out to be no big deal. He should have done it ages ago, and wasn't sure why he'd ever had any qualms about it. He hadn't been happy, he hadn't been happy for years, and it had nothing to do with his job, his house, or Alice, or even the poker, but because his brain wasn't doing its job properly. If you thought about it, it wasn't such a surprise – the human brain was the most complicated thing in the known universe. All of his computers and software programs had eventually broken down and got clogged up with viruses and data scraps, so wasn't it only to be expected that the brain should?

Whatever, one little pill a day, and now he was sorted. Yes, it really was as simple as that. There had been no need for a ruinously expensive Swiss sanatorium, no highly dangerous electroshock treatment and, best of all, he hadn't had to visit some embarrassingly pretty psychotherapist one afternoon a week for year after year, in order to catalogue all of his personal and physical failings in the bleak hope that talking about it would somehow make the problems go away. As if that was likely to happen – you would do just as well to get down on your knees and pray to the moon.

The pills weren't like cocaine or anything, not that he'd ever tried it of course. They didn't make you feel brilliant, they just stopped you feeling shit all the time, and they took the twitchiness away. Alan hadn't found the secret of happiness, but he had found the secret of not being unhappy – it was just a matter of getting the neurochemical balance right. After all, the mind is just the brain, and the brain is just the sum of ten billion fizzing and sparking neurons, endlessly spitting out their potassium and sodium ions to one another, and as long as enough of them were doing this in approximately the right way, life was OK. He didn't know why the government didn't just put the stuff in the water, like fluoride. There were some side effects, of course, but nothing to worry about, and one of them was that he had now become good at poker.

'Five pounds,' said Simon.

'Call,' said Alan.

'I'm in for five,' said Doug.

'Call,' said Nick.

'Fold,' said Vijay.

Vijay dealt the fourth card on to the table. There was now a four of diamonds, a five of hearts, a jack of spades and a two of diamonds on the table. Nick had the three and jack of clubs in his hand. An ace or a six on the final card would give him a straight. Well, that had to be worth staying in for, but what were those bastards going to do? It was five to twelve, this would be the last hand of the night. So far, he'd been doing fantastically well, God he had practically *broken even*, and if he could take the last pot it would make it the most successful evening he'd had for over a year. But first he had to win it.

'Two pounds,' said Simon.

'Fold,' said Alan.

OK, good – one down. He could do without Alan sticking this one out, given the way he'd been playing. Simon was still in, which was never good, but he didn't seem to be betting with any great ambition. Though of course with Simon you never knew what was going on.

'See your two and raise another eight,' said Doug.

This was it. How brave was Nick feeling? More importantly, how lucky was he feeling? He didn't need to do any calculations to know that the wise thing, almost certainly, was to fold now. To finish the evening without loss, to make sure it ended so very differently from the last time. Did he really have the appetite for this?

'Call ten pounds, and raise another ten,' said Nick.

'Fold,' said Simon.

Doug paused for a moment, and fixed his gaze on Nick. He'd been prepared for this, and he calmly stared back. For what seemed an extraordinary length of time, but was probably no more than five seconds, they looked into each other's eyes. Nick didn't flinch.

'OK, I'll call your ten pounds. Let's see what the last card gives us.'

Vijay dealt the fifth card and, thank the fucking heavens to Christ, it was the ace of hearts! He'd done it! He had the fucking straight! He had held his nerve and he had been rewarded.

Doug wasn't going to beat that – surely not this time. He checked the cards on the table again. The flush was impossible, the full house was impossible and, of course, four of a kind was impossible, as if that was ever going to happen again. OK, as straights go Nick had the lowest possible, running from ace low to five, but surely that didn't matter? Doug could only beat him if he had the three and six in his hand for the higher straight, and he didn't – not a chance. It wasn't even a matter of probabilities – he *didn't*.

Nick could see that Doug could see that Nick knew. That was a shame – it meant that he wasn't going to expensively try to bluff his way out of it. The game was over, there was no more money to be won, but they still had to go through the formalities.

'Check,' said Doug.

'Bet twenty pounds,' said Nick.

'Take it. It's yours, but by Christ you got lucky there.'

The more I practise, the luckier I get. Nick had seen the quote on Doug's study wall, and it had always struck him as exactly the kind of brainless and false thing that Doug would think. Although, maybe now he ought to reconsider a bit. For what had Nick been doing these last few months except practising? Whatever the blows, whatever shit and extraordinary thing happened to him, he had kept going. He had doubted, but he had never wavered in his mission, and the result was that he had been blessed with some luck at long last. Sophia McLain was a huge slice of good luck, there was no doubt about it, but it was up to him to make the most of it. *Fortune favours the brave* – wasn't that another of the fucking stupid things that Doug liked to say from time to time? Well, it was time to be brave.

Round at Vijay's – October

'So what books do you like reading yourself?'

As opening lines go, it was hardly the most scintillating, and that was after a week and a half of thinking about it. But actually, it wasn't the worst way to begin. Books, after all, were what they had in common – he taught them and she read them. Also, as with all the best questions in these kinds of situations, Nick already knew the answer. He knew exactly what kind of books she read and while, obviously, he couldn't bear them, he was hardly going to tell her that. There were times when it was useful, indeed essential, that you disagreed violently about books, and others when it was more important to warmly nod your agreement and approval. This was one of those.

It was poker night. Nick was in the Entropy, a wine bar on Church Road. Earlier that afternoon, coughing theatrically into the mouthpiece, Nick had rung Vijay and given him the bad news. For the first time in the history of their games, he was not going to be able to make it. The flu doing the rounds at school had finally caught up with him, and he was laid up in bed feeling thoroughly miserable. An enormously disappointed Vijay had kindly wished him well. Two hours later, Janet had wished him luck as he had left for his game. Even allowing for the thing with Doug and the drugs, it was arguably the most dishonest thing he'd ever done. Which if you thought about it, over the course of a lifetime, wasn't really all that bad. Although strangely, and he wasn't sure what this signified, it had felt worse lying to Vijay than it had to Janet.

It was Sophia who had proposed that they meet, and suggested the date, and he had immediately agreed to the plan. He was hardly going to disagree with anything she said at this stage, but he'd also liked the elegance of it. There was a cold-hearted cunningness to the plan that had impressed him, and made him think that she must have done this kind of thing before. Well, he wasn't bothered about that. The main thing was that, at long last, he was going to fuck Doug at poker night, even if he wasn't actually there at the time. There was an awful lot to think and worry about with all this, but he had to try to keep that thought uppermost in his mind.

It had been his task to come up with a venue. That hadn't been easy. Reading was a small town and with something like this there were some obvious dangers. Even if he did want Doug to find out that his wife was being unfaithful, and he still wasn't sure what the long-term objective of all this was, it was important that it didn't happen yet, and that Doug didn't know it was with him. Then there was Janet, of course – it was absolutely imperative that she didn't find out about this. It would also be awkward if any of his colleagues saw him, and above all – he mustn't get seen by any of his pupils. Three years ago there had been a near-calamitous incident when a group of sixth formers had discovered him semi-unconscious on a park bench, and he had had to buy the little fuckers a bottle of vodka just to keep them quiet.

He was pleased with the place he'd finally selected. The Entropy was close to the university campus, on the east side of town, and far away from where any of Doug's business friends would be likely to turn up. Far away as well from anyone Nick knew, all of whom were teachers and tended to just slump into the nearest and cheapest pub they could find. The pupils were more problematic, those wankers tended to get everywhere, but no – this place seemed pretty safe, and expensive enough to deter them. The people here looked to be drawn from Reading's professional classes – some university types, maybe the odd doctor or lawyer. That was good, for alongside bumping into anyone they knew, they needed to avoid all the nutters and bastards that come out on a Friday night. After all, quite apart from anything else, it was going to be quite important that Sophia had a good time.

'So what about Greek writers, I mean modern ones. Are there any you would recommend?'

He took a gulp from his beer as she tried to answer his question as thoroughly as possible. Christ, that was appallingly wooden – where did that come from? What a hopeless thing to ask, and now she clearly felt as if she was being tested. He wasn't even interested in her answer – as if he was going to rush off to buy up the latest big thing in contemporary Greek fiction. He had to come up with something better than that.

One thing he hadn't been expecting, and which wasn't helping matters, was how nervous Sophia was. At home, she had always been so fuck-off imperious. Marching across the living room in high heels, throwing her head back to kindly acknowledge the boys with their card games, she had been something of a mystical figure, formidable and war-like, the mistress of the house and anything else she wanted. But now, up close and alone, much of her power had dissipated. It seemed that, after all, she was no more or less than a married woman in her forties who lived in Reading and liked books.

It should have been more easy-going than this, but he was still coming to terms with the difficulty that his original opening wasn't going to work, for the simple reason that she hadn't read the book he'd sent her. Of course, she was looking forward to reading it, and she said it looked interesting and intriguing, but she hadn't actually read so much as a single story. This had been a major blow. Nick had intended for Borges to get them through the first hour at least, and had carefully designed and rehearsed a brilliant series of speeches and supplementary riffs on the subject of Borges' concept of infinity and the complexities of self-referential identity. They were so good, in fact, that he was wondering if he should just say them anyway.

After all, what else was he going to talk about? Apart from books there wasn't that much that he was knowledgeable about, and the things that he very much wanted to discuss – what she thought of her husband, Doug's boorishness, her dissatisfactions and desires, and maybe even what she thought of *him* – were going to be off-limits for at least a couple of hours. He was trying to remember how he'd managed to charm and seduce Janet all those not terribly good years ago, but there wasn't much he could draw on. As far as he could recall, it hadn't required a huge amount of effort on his part. They had gone to the cinema and possibly even the theatre a few times, and he had doubtless said some clever and spiteful things about what they had seen, and then very quickly they had settled into a comfortable arrangement, whereby he hadn't been expected to do anything particularly spectacular, and she seemed perfectly willing to manage their lives.

And before Janet? Well, it wasn't as if there had been hundreds, but he had certainly had one or two girlfriends. The problem was that he'd never really gone on dates before, if that's what this was. His strategy had generally been to grind girls down, to impress and oppress them over cups of coffee, repeated meetings at the photocopier and drinks after work.

In this kind of arena, where you had no more than a few hours to make your mark and take your chance, and with little prospect of having another go at it the next day, he was much less sure of himself.

One thing he did have going in his favour was that, although not generally recognised, he was actually quite good-looking. There was a thoughtfulness about his eyes, a humbleness to his nose and even a delicateness to his small mouth which had come across as naive and unassuming when younger, but now gave him an unexpected freshness. Physically, it was hopeless, he was the very opposite of Doug – shortish, with sloping shoulders, thin arms and a cardiovascular system so decrepit that he could barely climb the stairs without panting. But you couldn't tell that just sitting in a pub, and at least he hadn't yet lost his hair or put on much weight. At least he had his luck to thank for that.

'So, have you ever done any writing? Creative writing, I mean. Did you ever want to be a writer yourself instead of just a –'

She left it there, awkwardly, but he had been expecting that one. The answer of course was no, he never had, for any number of reasons, but mainly because he was an awful writer. He hadn't necessarily always been, but all those years of studying post-structuralist texts, writing essays on semiotics and teaching modern fiction had given him the world view of Jack Kerouac and the prose style of Michel Foucault. Crucially, he was well aware of this, which meant that he had never done anything really stupid like go off to Nepal to write novels on top of mountains, or even just sit in the garden shed every evening, with a deranged sense of his own importance. He may not have discovered much about the world in his time here, but at least, after forty years, he knew his place in it.

'No,' he said. 'It's never been something that's interested me very much. There are more than enough books for me or anyone else to read, and I think the world is in need of more good readers than writers. In fact, I often think that reading well is almost as hard as writing well.'

It helped that he actually believed at least half of what he had just said. 'And what about you?' he said. 'Do you have ambitions of that kind?'

'No, no, not at all! I can't write a thing and wouldn't dream of trying! Actually, I really agree with you. When I used to teach, I always used to feel that it was the single most important thing in the world. Although, of course,' she added hastily, 'I was only teaching modern languages – not *literature*.'

She had been a teacher! He had never known that, or if he ever had then he'd forgotten. So they had something else in common. What was more, and this was both unusual and tremendously helpful, somehow she had never come to despise teachers. In fact, and this was barely credible, she seemed to think that they were *good people*. All the things he had once believed, or at least once tried to believe, she still seemed to think were true. Instead, her frustrations were with the bureaucracy, the constraints of the national curriculum, poorly defined performance metrics, and the impossibility of being creative in the classroom. Well, that was fine. He didn't really know where she was coming from with much of this, but he was happy to emphatically agree with her for the next half an hour or so, and to participate in a well-functioning conversation about how put-upon and bullied and poorly respected the profession had become. She was on to her second glass of wine now, and seemed to be gaining in confidence, which meant of course that he was.

Now that she was doing most of the talking, he was able to look at her more carefully. She wasn't as pretty as he had remembered. Perhaps that was why at Doug's she always tended to walk past so quickly – someone like Sophia would have an acute sense of how best she should be viewed, of the way that light and shadow and speed and angles and paint could conjure up the image she wanted for her audience. And there was no doubt she was impressive: her hair was very black, her lips red and her face very white, but close up, without the distance and height and majesty, it didn't work in the same way. She was a few years older than him of course. Not many, but enough for her skin to have congealed slightly and her eyes to look strained. What was also disappointing was that she didn't have even a trace of a Greek accent. In fact, it turned out she had been born in Swindon, and firmly sounded like it.

Also, she was terribly thin. Was she unhappy? There was a sorrowfulness about her that wasn't just self-pity, and which he found undeniably attractive – it more than made up for the accent. She wasn't depressed or fucked up or anything, not as far as he could tell, but there was an exquisite sadness there all the same. She had money and children of course, but maybe she was spiritually restless? Was she one of those women who spent all their time reading novels because their lives were so lacking in drama and emotional complexity? Well, he could certainly give her plenty of that.

'I'm just going out for a cigarette. Do you smoke?'

So she smoked. Now that really was something. Nick didn't smoke himself, but more to the point – Doug hated smoking. Along with paying taxes, it was one of his great bugbears. Surely he couldn't know that Sophia smoked? What other secrets did she have from him? He didn't go outside with her. He was a hopeless smoker, but maybe he should have – it could have been an opportunity for increasing the intimacy. But no – there was no need to hurry, better to go to the bar and get more drinks, and besides he needed the time to think of some more things to talk about.

It was ten minutes before she returned, and in that time something had clearly happened to her. Had she made her mind up about something, or spoken to someone on the phone, or had the cigarettes and alcohol and cold air made her light-headed? Because when she came back the first thing she did was reach for her glass and take a long, deep drink from it, as if it was a pint of beer rather than red wine.

And then she said, 'So what's Doug like at poker?'

'Oh, well, since you ask, actually he's not terribly good.' Again, this was a question he had been expecting, indeed hoping for, and he had a very clear idea of how to play it.

'Really? I thought he usually won. I'm sure he's always telling me about his little victories at cards.'

Nick smiled, happily noticing the edge of malice in her voice. 'I suspect all husbands tell their wives something similar. No. It's not as if he loses a fortune, but he nearly always ends up down by the end of the night. He tends to play a very straight game – he's easy to read, and not a terribly good bluffer. A good poker player needs to be more enigmatic.'

She nodded.

'Well, that fits,' she said. 'I suppose poker must be a good test of character, and that people must play poker in the same way they do everything else. You would hardly describe Doug as an enigma, and he's hopeless when it comes to decision-making.'

'But he's entrepreneurial,' said Nick, now completely thrilled, 'and very successful in business. I would have thought that he's very dynamic in the right situation.'

He knew it was important to defend Doug from this point onwards. At last she was starting to tell him what he had so wanted to hear, but it would have to be given rather than extracted. She was a proud woman, they all were, and, with any luck, she had all kinds of hateful and insightful criticisms to make about her husband, but she certainly wouldn't tolerate anyone else doing the same thing.

'But he's so *straight!* He's really a very unimaginative man. You know he's barely read a book in his life, unless it's something to do with sport. I'm sure he's a bad bluffer. You know he's a terrible liar – really no good at all. And he's such a coward too! He's terrified of Dad. And I wouldn't be too impressed by his business stories. It's the Lakises who run the thing now – Doug is really a sort of mascot, or at least, that's what he should be.'

To his own surprise, he was proving to be really quite good at this. He was nodding sympathetically, and making the kind of vaguely supportive noises and prompts that seemed to gently encourage her.

'Don't get me wrong, he's very hard-working – that's always been his big strength, or at least it used to be, and there's no doubt he was on to something when he first started up the health clubs. But he's out of his depth now in all sorts of ways. He's never been in the slightest bit strategic, that's part of the problem. He likes to talk about his instincts and his gut-feel for things, but you need more than that to run a business. I suppose that shows at poker as well.'

'Well, yes, and poker's essentially an analytical game. In fact, that's often the difference betwe–'

'And, of course, let's be honest – he's been amazingly lucky. He sort of inherited a gym in the 1990s, and rode the whole boom years, without ever quite knowing what he was doing. All of his dumb decisions, and there have been some really dumb ones, have paid off in the most unlikely of ways. Until now.'

'Well, you're right there. I've always considered Doug to be one of the luckiest men I've known, and for all sorts of reasons.' It hadn't been in the least bit necessary, but just to be absolutely sure, he had stared ineptly into her eyes as he had said this. She smiled warmly, a nice smile, though it was hard to know if he was being charming or embarrassing. She had, he noticed, exceptionally good teeth.

Sophia went on, and now Nick didn't need to say anything. He was no more than a bystander, as she thoroughly, even wittily, described the McLain household. Had she given this speech many times before? It was possible, there was a certain precision and competency to it. But Nick wasn't particularly bothered, he was far more interested in all the wonderful and surprising things she was telling him: that Doug was ferociously jealous of his brother who had once played rugby for Scotland; that her father considered him to be a philistine and an almost total idiot; that he had borrowed a stupid amount of money for his new club, which was now in danger of going bust before it even opened; and that their marriage was largely functional and joyless, despite Doug still being devoted to her.

In fact, and this was difficult to believe, it was almost *too* much. For Nick suddenly started to feel something that he'd never felt round the poker table. He started to feel sorry for Doug. He loved his wife, that was obvious, and his wife didn't seem to love him any more. Or at least, she didn't respect him and with a woman like Sophia the two things obviously went together. Wasn't that a sad and terrible thing? Was this really the time to be trying to ruin his life? Or was he just making the same mistake as countless other executioners and assassins? He knew that he had to keep a certain amount of distance, otherwise knowledge blurred into understanding and the monster stopped being monstrous.

Suddenly Sophia stopped. She shook her head. 'God. Let's not talk about Doug any more. Let's get some ouzo.'

Before he could say anything, she'd marched off to the bar. Well, it seemed that was all he was going to get from her on the subject of Doug. But that was fine – he had more than enough now, and he would have to set aside some time another day to collate and analyse and have qualms about it. Whatever happened next, the evening had already been at least half a success. Could it be anything else? Did he really *want* anything else? The only thing he knew for certain was that he didn't want the evening to end yet. They didn't have any ouzo, but she returned with a drink which, if anything, looked even more revolting – a black liquid with an ominous viscosity that sat unattractively at the bottom of the glass.

Laughing for no particular reason, they gulped it down together with a traditional Greek toast. He could feel it, warm and immobile in his stomach. He had possibly drunk too much tonight, but that was OK, that had been expected – he couldn't see any way round it, and had always known that intoxication would be a key element to his strategy. He went to buy some more drinks and chose something only marginally less idiotic and then, while she was out having another cigarette, he cautiously slipped into her glass some of the remaining MDMA. Not that this had ever really been part of the evening's plan, but somehow it suddenly seemed like a very good idea, and not that he had put much in, but hopefully it would be enough to get her going in some uninhibited and reckless way. And then, partly out of curiosity, but also to ensure that the moral consequences weren't quite so dire, he put some in his glass too.

Sure enough, forty minutes later, and he was certainly getting somewhere. Although he had to acknowledge it would have been something of a blow if he hadn't been. She clearly disliked her husband, she was riotously drunk and he'd fed her a load of drugs. Mercifully, they weren't affecting her like they'd affected Doug – she wasn't jumping on the table or doing any singing. But she was getting animated, and also, more interestingly, she was starting to get physically intimate. Actually, it was all very exciting. She was holding on tightly to his fingers and brushing her black hair against his. Clearly, things were going well. They weren't talking about Doug any more, they weren't really talking about anything.

He noticed that there were two women on the other side of the room who were staring fixedly at them. It was hard to say whether they were disapproving or possibly even enjoying the spectacle – after all, it was a fine sight, they were a fine couple. Just to show them, he gently took Sophia's hand and lightly kissed the tips of her fingers. She smiled and looked into his eyes. She seemed much younger now, the tiredness round the face had disappeared, her lips had darkened with red wine and her eyes had come alive. For this night at least, with nothing but his charms and some MDMA, he had wiped away her cares and made her young again. There was even, he was certain, a delightfully eccentric slice of Greek to her accent.

It was now half past twelve, which meant that he had been working up to this point for nearly five hours. Importantly, he was feeling fucking great. No wonder Doug had had the night of his life back in July – this stuff was brilliant. He was glowing, he was feeling energised and dynamic, in total control but also enjoyably out of control, and what's more, he looked marvellous. Staring into the mirror in the toilets, he had been mesmerised by his own beauty. He was so handsome it was joyful. That couldn't just be the drugs, surely, making him look like this? He certainly couldn't remember Doug looking particularly brilliant on them. No – it was him. All he had needed was to feel young again, to be himself, to feel like he never actually had done when he was young. What was Orwell's old line? *By the age of forty, you have the face you deserve*? Well, he was forty, and he too had the face he deserved. And it was a fucking good one.

He walked calmly, majestically back into the bar, where actually things had become a bit confusing. A set of important lights had come on, people were getting up to go, there were bags and coats being fetched and carried. A very large man with a small head had turned up and was issuing commands, but in a voice so loud that Nick couldn't understand what he was saying. He was finding it all a bit overwhelming, and there were some odd little trails of white light dancing in the corners of his eyes which he could see might be good fun, but for the moment were just adding to his difficulties. And then Sophia suddenly appeared right in front of him, with a wonderful kindly smile, and firmly led him out of the bar.

Surprisingly, it wasn't in the least bit cold outside. It was a pleasant evening and there was no need at all to go home just yet. Besides, he had just started saying the most interesting and incredible things. He was talking about Borges, he didn't know how it had come up, but he felt it was timely and important that it had. He had already started explaining to Sophia why Borges' notion of randomness was more of a metaphysical than a statistical construction, when she put her finger lightly up to his lips and said, 'It's OK, you can stop talking now. I already like you.'

And then, without waiting for an answer, she had kissed him. It was a perfect kiss, comprehensive and confident, but also soft, without any force or strain to it. Clearly, she had done this many times before, and not just with Doug. Now it was his turn to kiss her and it was, in comparison, a bit all over the place. In fact, he barely managed to connect with her lips at all. It didn't matter in the least, that was another good thing about the drugs, and anyway he was in expert hands.

She steered him backwards, out of the doorway and along to the car park. Unfortunately, neither of them actually had a car, but there was a wall at least, and now he was pinned up against it. Sophia was pressing firmly into him, holding his face in her hands, and repeatedly kissing him.

And then, no more than two or three minutes later, she unexpectedly stopped kissing him and said, 'That's enough now. I need to get home.' There was no pleading or longing, he knew a teacher's voice when he heard it, and it required compliance.

He pulled back and tried to look into her face. There was nothing coquettish or charming about the way she was looking at him. In fact, for a moment, she didn't even look as if she liked him very much. It was late, it was cold, the drugs had worn off, and she wanted to get back to her husband. He wondered for a moment if he should try to sexually assault her. But no – he was a teacher, for fuck's sake, and besides she was as tall as he was and almost certainly in much better physical condition. In any case, he didn't feel like it, and he had a strong sense that that kind of thing was something you couldn't really attempt half-heartedly.

She walked past him, back through the car park and on to the street. Not knowing what else to do, he followed her for ten yards until she stopped abruptly under a street light.

'Are you OK?' he said.

'Yes, I'm fine, thanks. Sorry – it's been really fun. Really, I've had a great night. But I have to get home now. It's so late. I hope you understand.'

He nodded. They kissed each other twice again, politely on each cheek, as if it was the beginning of the evening rather than the end. He made a feeble offer to find her a taxi home, but she clearly wanted to get quickly away and strode off into the night and, even though he needed to go in the same direction, he turned the other way.

Now that he was on his own and his mind had calmed down, he could think. Although he had learnt a lot more about Doug, he still knew almost nothing about Sophia, except that she used to be a teacher and was a bit fucking crazy. How come she had been so nervous? And then later so incredibly professional? Had it been bewildering and shocking for her, or the kind of thing she did all the time? Well, one thing was for sure – at the very least, he would have to describe the evening as a major success. Either that or a total disaster. Technically, had he just committed adultery? Surely you had to do more than just that? It certainly didn't feel like any great crime, though it might well do tomorrow. In any case, as an intelligence-gathering exercise, it had unquestionably achieved its objectives, and there could be no doubt that he had got one over on Doug, big time, even if he must never ever know. But was that enough? Mission creep had set in, and now, at the end of the evening, he seemed to want different things than he had at the beginning. Or had he always wanted them? And what did he want to happen next? Could Sophia be depended upon to be sensible – did he want her to be? Christ, this was difficult: the situation was fast-moving, the information imperfect and the motives unclear. It was worse than fucking *poker*, and he never even won at that. But he had to keep it together – whatever happened now, it was vital that events remained under his control and nobody else's.

Simon stubbed out his cigarette. He was just ten more minutes' walk from home. It had in many ways been a frustrating night. No Nick, of course, which meant that the table had been missing its principal sucker. Alan couldn't be relied upon any more – in fact, he'd had another good evening. Vijay hadn't played well, as always studying the cards but not the players, but even so – you were never going to get rich off the back of Vijay. So it had been down to Doug, who hadn't been on his game at all. But even so – Doug was no Nick, worse luck, and Simon had finished the evening just twenty pounds up. If he had taken a taxi back, then half of that would have gone. It had hardly been a good use of his time.

But perhaps the evening wasn't quite over yet, because he was now watching something quite extraordinary going on. For there, directly across the road from him, were Nick and Sophia McLain. There was no mistaking them, they were actually quite close and he had a clear view of them under the street light. Instinctively, Simon stepped back, out of the light, but he barely needed to bother. They weren't in any kind of state to notice him. Hellishly drunk by the looks of things, and Christ – Nick looked absolutely *terrible*. What on earth had he been doing to himself?

They were up close and talking. He couldn't hear what they were saying, but whatever it was, they didn't speak for long. Clearly, whatever they had been up to this evening was coming to an end. Turning abruptly, she had gone one way and he the other. Could it really be possible that they were having an affair? Sophia with *Nick* of all people? How could that have possibly happened? Well, he wasn't about to find out now, and anyway the question wasn't *why* – he had wasted most of his life with such unfathomable lines of enquiry. No, the real question was what was he going to do about it.

At the Transcontinental
Hotel – November

Nick drove into the Transcontinental car park warily. It was on the outskirts of Reading, on the west side, the part of town that he knew least about and feared the most. The part of town that hadn't so much grown as just appeared – a mysterious grid of business parks, underutilised dual carriageways, mini roundabouts, conference centres and health clubs that never used to be here but now, indisputably, were. No one would ever call it futuristic, it wasn't that interesting, but it was the future, anyone could see that. It was half past seven, but the car park was sufficiently well lit for him to quickly establish that his car was the smallest and oldest there.

He picked his way along an illuminated pathway, threaded between low hedges and bare flowerbeds, until he found his way to the hotel reception. This only made him more anxious. The hotel was a huge, bloated affair. Not simply a place for people to sleep in but to do all manner of other things as well. There was a restaurant, piano bar and wireless-internet business centre, there was a gym with squash courts, there were training suites and high-end retail outlets.

The disarmingly young man at reception wordlessly directed Nick to some steps. Nick walked down and across the bar, feeling ill at ease and stared at. It was a long way from the Rose and Crown, and he was hardly the lord of this domain. Just like his car, he was the oldest and smallest there. Reaching the bar at last, he sat down on a leather stool and carefully surveyed the room. It was large, generous and comfortable with a low window running right across the far wall and, in the opposite corner, a handsome grand piano. Young men and women were hunched around small glass tables, or else sitting back reading newspapers in wicker armchairs and impractical window seats. Beneath the soft but purposeful chatter, he could hear the faint hum of the motorway traffic.

Once upon a time, Reading had been a railway town, one of those places that sales reps from London companies would stop off at, on their way to Swindon, Oxford and Bristol, and try to sell agricultural machinery and engineering parts to local farms and businesses. The days of travelling salesmen had, he supposed, long gone and with them had gone all sorts of other things that he had never liked much but now felt an inexplicable fondness for – smoking indoors and having four sugar lumps in tea, playing games in pubs and telling jokes about Irishmen. And people didn't work in sales any more – they worked in *business development*, and they weren't reps but *consultants*. In fact, everyone nowadays, apart from the teachers, was a fucking consultant. Nor did they carry flimsy brochures or give out company pens, they went around with beautiful silver-and-black laptop computers and sat in places like this, fiddling about with PowerPoint and making authoritative graphs and pie charts.

As he sat at the bar, looking at them out of the side of his eyes, he could see they were energised and alert – professionally competent, enthusiastic about their jobs, physically at ease with themselves and almost certainly good at poker. Lots of them, he noticed darkly, seemed to be drinking mineral water. This recession was long overdue, in fact it could do with hurrying up a bit, for these were all Doug's people – not his rugby or business mates, but the kind of people he had built his empire on. These were the foot soldiers of the New Economy, the business-park crowd, the new generation of managers and wealth-takers, and he badly wanted to make himself feel superior to them. An economic slump, a major contraction in financial and business services or any other industrial sector apart from teaching, would certainly help.

He had now been there for thirty minutes. He had expected Sophia to be late, but of course that didn't mean that he could risk being late as well. And anyway, it had given him the opportunity to think things through a bit. He certainly needed it. He had seen her just once since their night in the pub. She had come to the first evening class and been its undoubted star: she had sat at the front, she seemed to have read everything on the reading list and the many things she said were intelligent, but also insightful in ways that suggested she hadn't just looked up some things to say on the internet, which was what Nick himself usually did. She hadn't come for a drink afterwards, but she had lingered to thank him and tell him how much she'd enjoyed the class, and to ask some perceptive questions about the assignment he'd set.

So that was all encouraging. And then, just three days ago, she had emailed him. A short, breezy email that he'd read about forty times and still couldn't make any sense of. It was intelligible of course – an enquiry into his well-being and a straightforward, friendly request to see him again. But what did she really want from all this? *Why* did she want to see him? To carry on where they left off last time, to sadly explain why they must never meet again, or did she just want to talk some more about her homework? Or maybe it was simply that she was lonely, Nick was friendly and she didn't want to spend the evening with her husband?

And why did he want to see her? That question was at least as troubling. The idea, all those months ago, had been to destroy Doug, and it had undoubtedly provided him with a much needed purpose and sense of identity. What he was far less certain about was *why* he was doing it. Nor was he at all sure whether this was part of the same plan. Hadn't he collected enough evidence? Hadn't he done enough to be able to sit down at the table with Doug and skilfully bring about his downfall, if that's what he still wanted? Surely he didn't have to do anything else now. So if this was no longer about Doug, then why had his heart jumped when he'd received her email? Why had he spent thirty minutes on his two-sentence reply? And, above all, why the fuck was he here?

Still no sign of her. It was a quarter past eight. What with all this analysis, unhelpful doubts were beginning to bubble up. Was this a set-up of some kind? Was it a trick? Was he just going to sit here all evening and then go home? Or maybe Doug had somehow intercepted her email and had her chained up in the cellar? Christ, worse still, what if it was actually *Doug* who had emailed him, and was now making his way over here for a violent confrontation. He ordered another drink, he needed to calm down a bit. But he had to watch it, and there would be no funny business this time – no exotic liquors and certainly no mucking about with drugs. No, he had to stay focused and on top of things, disciplined and clear-headed. He would stick with orange juice and vodka, and nothing else, and he'd keep a careful count of them.

Sophia had selected the venue, and he still hadn't even begun to work out what it signified. Obviously, it was a hotel, which meant that it was full of rooms and beds, but she couldn't surely be intending for them to use one? More likely it was the remoteness of the place that explained why they were meeting here. There certainly wasn't much chance of bumping into anyone they knew from Reading. Surely not even any of those gobshites from school were going to make it out here. But was that really the reason? Nick had always been stronger on the symbolic analysis. He might not be able to discern any rational objectives behind Sophia's decision to meet here, or other people's poker bets come to that, but he could expertly size up what a place stood for. He could sense its godless contingency, the unbroken corporate facelessness, and the peculiar way in which nobody knew anyone. Whether it was the hotel staff, bussed in and out by the temping agency, or the guests he was looking at now, the professionals who worked alongside one another, drank bottled water in the bar and played squash together, *nobody knew anyone*. The place was designed to host business deals, to hold management-training workshops and to have affairs in, for people to meet and briefly interact, possibly pleasurably and possibly not; for them to bounce into and off one another, like the molecules in all those glasses of carbonated water.

God – an *affair*. Was that really what he was embarking on? He wasn't in the least bit sure that that's what he wanted. What had happened to his moral high ground? Although, at least on this occasion, he hadn't needed to lie to anyone. It didn't necessarily make the situation any better, but it had certainly made it easier. Janet was away for the evening, back in Staffordshire, staying with cousins and then visiting her mother at the nursing home. It was a trip that Nick had managed to get out of weeks ago, by making some credible excuses about work commitments. But that wasn't the same thing as lying about meeting up with Sophia. He felt reasonably confident about that.

Even so, whether he was lying to Janet or not, he couldn't help but feel that he was entering a new, ethically problematic subculture. He'd never explored it before himself, he'd never been to this hotel or had to secretly arrange meeting places, but it all felt very familiar. He'd read enough novels, seen enough television dramas and knew enough teachers to recognise it. This was what happened to men and women in their forties, annihilated by their jobs, stupefied by their families, pincered between their domestic grumbles and existential fears. And he could see that it must be easier than it ever had been. Password-protected email accounts, text messaging, internet message boards, out-of-town conferences and hotel complexes. Would these be the building blocks of his new life? He wasn't sure how much he was going to like it. No doubt his life lacked something, but was this really it?

No, it wasn't, and in a moment of dramatic clarity, Nick suddenly knew that the thing to do was to fold. It's what Simon would have done, and Vijay would have long ago calculated that the odds and the prize and the dangers didn't add up. The smart play was to put down his drink, and get out of this horrible place. He could email her later, make up some excuse, lie for the right reasons for once, drive back home while possibly still under the limit, drink a bottle of red wine and fall asleep on the sofa. Anything else was madness. He got up from his bar stool and reached for his jacket and, just as he did so, Sophia walked in, smiling and apologising as she hurried across the room.

Nick sat back down. She looked great. Had she made an extra effort this evening? Was that why she was so late? Or was it the venue that suited her so well, with its warm lighting and soft, non-reflective surfaces? Or maybe it was just that, for whatever reason, she looked happy. She kissed him on the cheek, still smiling, and sat down next to him.

'So sorry, you must have been here for ages,' she said.

'No, no. I haven't been here long at all. Can I get you a drink?'

'Oh yes, but just a small glass of dry white wine. Last time you got me drinks I really don't know what happened.'

'Uh – yes, well. We probably did get a bit carried away.'

'Oh my God, yes. Sorry I had to leave in such a rush, but my head was spinning. I felt *awful* the next day. The whole weekend was a disaster. I've never felt anything like it. I had no idea a hangover could be like that.'

Nick nodded, and hastily tried to attract the barman's attention. If he had learnt just one thing this year it was that his experiments in spiking people with dangerous drugs were over. Although the idea hadn't been completely without merit, it was clear that the consequences couldn't be easily controlled and had every chance of being counter-productive. Also, apart from anything else, it was bang out of order.

'Oh good, I haven't missed anything. Dominic is just about to start.'

Looking across the room, Nick noticed for the first time that the piano at the far end of the bar had had its cover removed, and a young man in a suit far too big for him was now sitting there, massaging and flexing his hands. So was that why she had chosen this place? Because of the *pianist*? She didn't fancy him, did she? No, Nick didn't think she could. Dominic wasn't all that, for one thing, a music student probably, far too young and skinny. More likely, it was just as she said – she liked his playing, and didn't have anything else to do. In his head he quickly constructed a vision of Sophia driving out here on Saturday nights, Doug at home watching the football on television, and her sitting at the bar alone, drinking a single overpriced glass of house white wine, making small talk with the adolescent bar manager and listening to Dominic play the piano. God, and he thought *his* life was bleak.

'It's so good to hear proper music. You know Doug doesn't listen to anything, except rock music in the car. It's horrendous.'

Nick murmured in sympathy and shook his head. Although actually, music wasn't something that he knew much about. In the 1980s, living in London, he had gone to gigs in pubs where people loudly strummed guitars and hit drums, and shouted about how much they hated the government. He had grown out of that, but he'd never managed to grow into anything else. Jazz, for instance, which so many male teachers seemed to be fond of, was a tuneless mystery to him. The problem was that, unlike lots of other things, not knowing anything about music didn't mean that he could just write the whole thing off. Well, that wasn't completely true – it was probably safe to dismiss contemporary pop, folk music, hip hop, rap and reggae without ever listening to any of it, but classical music was a different thing entirely. He could hardly go around bragging that he didn't know anything about Bach.

Instead, he decided to move the conversation on to more familiar territory. 'And how is Doug?' he said.

The reassuring answer was that he hadn't got any better. Quite the opposite in fact, which probably had something to do with Sophia arranging this so hastily. Sophia gave Nick a detailed update on her husband's recent insensitivities and blunders. It seemed to Nick that Sophia had reached a significant stage in her feelings towards Doug. It was no longer just a matter of feeling fed up, irritated, bored or neglected. There was scorn and a deadly contempt in the way she talked about him. Hadn't he seen it himself, months ago, when she'd laughed at Doug for not having read his books? Nick was hardly an expert, but it seemed to him that contempt was one of the few things that a marriage really couldn't survive.

The pianist stopped abruptly. Was that the end? He knew it was often hard to tell with this sort of music. Sure enough, just as he was about to start clapping, Dominic was off again. Even if Nick couldn't tell if it sounded good or not, he certainly looked the part. There was a profound serious-ness to his performance – combining a surly demeanour with an extravagance to his gestures and flourishes, all elbows and hands, which looked theatrical and inefficient, but just short of ridiculous. Nick remembered suddenly why he'd stopped listening to music – it was because of the fucking musicians.

'And what about you?' said Sophia. 'How is everything? How's school? The winter term does drag on so. And how are they getting on with *Richard II*?'

Nick looked at her carefully, maybe even oddly. It was the kindest thing that anyone had said to him in months. For one thing, to his astonishment, she had remembered what he was teaching his A level class. He couldn't recall having told her, in fact some mornings he struggled to remember himself. But it was more than that. She actually seemed to be *interested* in him. Interested in his welfare, what he was doing and how he was feeling. Why? Why on earth would anyone behave like that?

Not quite sure what he was doing, he started to answer her question truthfully. He would *declare his hand*. She had asked him how everything was and he would tell her. He would tell her how it was rather than how he wished it was. It wasn't like a conversation with Janet, where they would exchange infor-mation on no more than the subjects that they both needed to know about, and it wasn't like chatting round the poker table, or the pub after the evening classes. There was no bluffing. He didn't talk about Borges, he didn't deliver any well-rehearsed speeches about modernist literature or make clever, savage remarks about popular culture. No, he told her about his job and how demoralising it was, how he disliked his colleagues and had stopped caring for the pupils. He told her about his house, about the treacherous boiler, the black furniture, the calamity of the ProPokerPlus! and his stupid works of art. He talked about living in London for all those years. He didn't give her the standard version, which was based around a melo-dramatised series of entertaining misadventures and comic escapades. Instead he told her about where he had lived and how lonely he had been.

He was, he knew, exposing himself, but for some reason he didn't feel in the least bit vulnerable. He felt secure, as if the more he told her, the safer and closer he was to her. Christ – how many vodkas had he had? No, no more than three, it couldn't be that. And anyway, this didn't feel like that other, more famil-iar, type of confidence. It was more than having had plenty to drink, or sitting on a full house. This was a kind of calm, inner confidence that came from himself, from *being* himself, rather than from what he owned or what he'd drunk. Maybe this was what it was like being Alan, now that he was on those tablets.

Sophia was different as well, not like she'd been in the pub that night. She didn't seem nervous of him or unsure of herself. And it wasn't like the other times, when he'd seen her at home, striding forcefully through the rooms of her enor-mous house. Tonight, she was neither fearful nor fearsome. Which meant, of course, that there was much less need for Nick to either brag or be bashful. She talked a lot as well. Not just about Doug, but other things. Things that Nick wasn't interested in, but for some reason still liked hearing about. She told him about her childhood, how her mother had died young and how her father had bullied his son but adored his daughter. She told him stories about the summer holidays she used to spend in Cyprus with her grandmother, learning how to make hummus and bake honey cakes.

When she did start talking about Doug again, it wasn't as brutally as before. For some reason, Nick didn't mind that so much either. With his new confidence, he could afford to be more generous. It seemed that Doug, though Nick should have guessed this, was a brilliant father. With Alexis he played tag rugby in the park and gave him tennis lessons; and with Olympia he would spend Saturday mornings escorting her around the shopping centres, shrewdly advising her on her choice of trainers and pencil cases, and on Sunday afternoons he earnestly attended her tea parties in the playroom, sitting politely alongside her dolls and teddies as she served them plastic platefuls of plastic cake. And at least once a week, Doug would end up sleeping in the bunk bed with one or other of them, rescuing them from their childish nightmares.

Sophia went on. She was haunted by the fear that she wasn't a good mother. For some reason, she wasn't sure why, maybe to do with never having known her own mother, her maternal instincts were underdeveloped. She found the children hard work; their foibles and antics exasperated when she knew they ought to delight. She tended to snap at them, and she couldn't make them laugh like Doug. Whenever one of them banged their head or grazed their leg it was always their father they cried out for, never their mother – that wasn't normal, was it? It was hard for Nick to know or even see what she was worried about – there was certainly nothing especially delightful about the ones at school. But it was important to Sophia, he could see that, and that meant that it should also be important to him.

Looking at his watch, Nick was surprised to see that they had been talking together for two hours. The pianist had stopped, and the bar was deserted. It hadn't mattered that he didn't know anything about classical music, or that he'd only had four drinks. They hadn't run out of things to say to each other, and the pauses in their conversation had been tender rather than awkward. The barman stood, looking sullen and bored, pouring himself glasses of lemonade and wishing they would leave. Well, maybe they should.

It was at this point that Nick decided to take the very riskiest of chances. As with all his bets, however large, he didn't spend too long trying to assess the odds and outcomes. Besides, in this case they really were incalculable. It *felt* right, that had to be the main thing.

Taking care not to look her too closely in the eyes, he softly said, 'Would you like to come upstairs with me?'

There was a long pause, longer even than waiting for Vijay's deliberations at the poker table. But this was, he knew, a big call and he shouldn't be disheartened by the time she took over it.

'Yes,' she said at last. 'I would.'

Immediately Nick went back to the hotel lobby to book a room. His heart was pounding. At the reception he spoke with a young girl completely unfamiliar with how her computer worked, and who was unable to verify if there were any rooms available until her manager returned. He wanted very much to kill her. Five, six minutes later and he turned up at last. He was barely any older than she was, the whole fucking place was run by children, but he was at least able to identify one last room on the sixth floor. It had twin single beds and would cost a bewildering £210.

Fucking hell. Well, he could hardly go back and tell Sophia that it was all off. And he certainly couldn't tell her that it was too expensive. He'd made his play and he would have to see it through, and at least things with Janet hadn't got so bad that she went through his credit-card bills. He rushed back to the bar. He was horribly nervous and overexcited. What had happened to all of his inner calm? Fuck, he knew he should have had more to drink.

In the lift on the way up together, they didn't know what to say to each other. In fact, they didn't seem able even to look at one another, and instead just stared ahead at the steel panels. They emerged, immediately disorientated, on to a long, badly lit corridor with dark carpets and identical blond-wood doors. The signage was insufficiently unambiguous, and they set off in search of their room in the wrong direction.

It was another five minutes before they found it. The hotel was every bit as vast as it had seemed from the outside, and room number 625 was located at the furthest end of the south-west corridor. The whole situation required strong leadership. The room was on the corner of the building and oddly shaped and overheated, and in order to push the beds together he had to move a side table and unplug a lamp. Sophia mean-while stood against the wall, holding her handbag and looking frightened. Hadn't she done this before? He should have asked her earlier; he didn't dare to now.

'Would you like something from the minibar?'

She shook her head. That was discouraging – he needed her to say yes to things. Events were slipping away from him. Had he done anything wrong? The possibility should never be discounted, but on this occasion he didn't think so. It wasn't as if he'd really done anything, but the intimacy in the bar just fifteen minutes ago now seemed to have belonged to a differ-ent night, to different people. He needed to regain it – God, he had to do *something*. They couldn't just stand facing one another like idiots. He walked over to her, he calmly took the bag out of her hand and put it on the bed, and then, gently hold-ing her head, he kissed her carefully on the lips. That seemed to do the trick – at least up to a point. It wasn't like before, outside the pub, when she had initiated things, he didn't feel her surging into him, but there again she wasn't pushing him away and nor was she limp and absent, which was what he had been most dreading. She was cautiously pressing herself closer to him, and her arms were no longer hanging joylessly at her sides, but had come round his back and were tentatively hugging him.

OK, so far so good. They held one another like this for what felt a long time. Sophia was going along with all this, but clearly he would have to lead. She still had her coat on for one thing, and she gave him little assistance as he tugged at her sleeves and slipped it from her shoulders. But at least it was off. Then, firmly turning her round and away from the wall, he walked her across the room until she fell backwards on to the bed.

Now he was above her, hovering inches from her face and kissing down into her mouth. She was hesitantly kissing him back now. Was she enjoying this? It was hard to tell. He hadn't really expected her to giggle or smile much, but it was troubling, all the same, quite how serious she seemed. Maybe this was just how she was, maybe her sombreness signified intense physical and emotional pleasure. If only he'd slept with more Greek women, if only he'd slept with more *women*, then he would have had a better idea. Well, it was too late to worry about that now. He unclasped her two hair clips and unfurled her hair. At least that made her look more relaxed.

And then, for the first time in twenty minutes, Sophia spoke. 'If you're going to do anything, then you'll need protection. Have you got any condoms?'

Fail to prepare, then prepare to fail – wasn't that what you got taught by the sports masters at certain schools – Doug's, for instance? No, Nick did not have any fucking condoms. He'd been married for nearly a decade, why would he have? What an incredible oversight, but there again, to be fair, he'd never reckoned on it coming to this. Never mind, all was not lost. It needn't be a problem, he'd just get some, that was all. How hard could it be? The hotel had everything else.

In any case, Sophia now wanted a shower. Fine. That should give him enough time. Promising to be back in ten minutes, he kissed her good-humouredly on the eyes and nose, and left the room. Remembering to remember the way back, he made his way along the dark corridor to the lifts and down to the ground floor.

His best chance had to be a vending machine in the toilets. That was where people used to get them, and surely things hadn't changed so very much in the last ten years? He dashed back across the reception, through the bar and into the Gents. No, nothing there. His mind was racing. He could drive to the nearest garage, though that would present certain practical and legal challenges. But wait – he wasn't going to give up on this place just yet. The bar was empty, but the barman was still there. What did he have to lose?

'Excuse me,' he said. 'I don't suppose you've got any condoms you'd be prepared to let me have?'

Ordinarily, in these kinds of situations, it was meant to be the other way round. It was meant to be the callow, unsophisticated and ill-organised youth who nervously approached his vastly more knowing and experienced counterpart. The barman, like everyone else here, couldn't be any more than twenty years old. Not that he seemed disturbed by the question, or in the least bit intimidated by Nick, because patting his trouser pocket he said, 'I've got a packet of two in my wallet. You can have it for twenty quid.'

Nick stared hard into the young man's eyes. What the fuck had happened to this country? It wasn't his world any more, he knew that. He'd known it for some time. No wonder he was so poor and always lost at poker. It wasn't just that the future didn't have any space for him, the future didn't *like* him. It belonged to the blank-eyed juvenile behind the bar, to the precocious bastards at his school, to Alexis McLain, to the business-development managers, all of whom were catching up with him, but wouldn't simply overtake him – no, they were going to run him down.

'Christ. OK,' said Nick. 'It's a deal.' What choice did he have? He could hardly complain to the manager.

So he had the condoms. Whatever they'd cost, that was a major achievement. He could go back upstairs. Sophia would have showered and would be in bed waiting for him. All he had to worry about now was Doug's remarkable cock, which despite his best efforts had been looming uncomfortably in the back of his mind for much of the last half-hour.

'Wait,' he said. 'Can I get a double vodka? Just straight, no ice.'

Now he was ready. He slammed the glass on to the bar, gave the barman a curt nod, and marched back towards the reception. And to think that, just a few hours ago, he'd been on the point of folding! Well, he had raised, and raised again, and now look where he was! The future was mediocre and would destroy him, and the past, the twentieth century, was now lost, and none of the causes had turned out to be worth fighting for anyway. But the present, this moment, was his. Politicians could talk about the future, but his was the tense of the romantic poet and he would be ensnared by no one else's rhetoric. If need be, he could live without consequence, he could *thrive* without it, in the moral universe that he alone created and ruled. He rode the lift upstairs, and tramped past the rooms of consultants, who had all finished their mineral waters and sensibly, miserably taken themselves off for an early night. Without even looking at the useless signage, he confidently slipped through the dark corridors, instinctively picking out his path. He knocked once, and then opened the door on to room 625.

It was empty, of course. He knew within less than a second. She wasn't in the shower or lying under the covers – there was no one there. The room was as orderly and lifeless as it had been when they'd gone in together, not half an hour ago. He checked the bathroom and it was clear that she hadn't used it – she had probably left the room just a minute after he had. He couldn't even begin to think *why* – there were too many reasons.

He sat down on the bed. He was overwhelmed by a cognitive storm, a deluge of thoughts and feelings, some complex and some very simple, which he was finding it difficult to process all at once. There was a smothering befuddlement and stupidity, a pang of sorrow and loss, a monstrous hollowness, a prickling of humiliation and shame, the odd flash of anger and smarting pain, an intense dizziness which could just be the vodka, and, also, beneath everything else, a faint but growing sense of relief.

Well, one thing was clear – he wasn't going anywhere else tonight. He'd paid for the room, and he was going to use it, though it was going to be difficult to see how he would ever get his money's worth out of all this. He crawled over to the minibar, and pulled out a tiny bottle of whisky, a can of Coca-Cola and a bag of peanuts. According to the helpful rate card, this would cost twelve pounds fifty, but he would worry about that tomorrow. He would worry about everything tomorrow.

Round at Simon's – November

Following Aristotle, who as far as Simon was concerned was the last person to have had anything remotely interesting to say on the subject, it was possible to divide humanity into four distinct types of moral being. There was the virtuous, the continent, the incontinent and the vicious.

With the virtuous character, his desires are in accordance with his decisions and actions, and those actions are the morally correct ones. The continent, too, also does the right thing, but in this case he has to go against his desires not to. In literary terms, this is the modern hero – the individual who triumphs in a moral conflict. By contrast, the incontinent is unable to suppress his desires. Despite knowing that he is doing the wrong thing, he will still go ahead and do it. He is an anti-hero. And finally, we have the vicious character, whose decisions are both immoral and consistent with his desires. In this case, there is no compunction about doing the wrong thing and no moral struggle. One would say that he is a villain.

Was Simon vicious? Was he the villain in all this? He didn't think so. Surely, to use an old philosopher's trick, the fact that he was even pondering the question demonstrated that he couldn't simply be described as vicious. But there again, given that he was considering blackmailing someone, possibly a friend, it was difficult to see his role as especially heroic. So did that mean he was morally incontinent? Anti-hero was better, but still – it wasn't a description he liked very much.

The issue would be less problematic if there was a Christian God, a divine being capable of making infallible distinctions and judgements on matters such as this. But Simon was a philosopher and could no more believe in an omnipotent and benevolent God than a geographer could believe that the earth was flat. Quite apart from anything else, if he were to start talking about Christianity in a philosophy lecture it really would be the end of his career. Although, as a matter of fact, he actually, secretly, did believe in God, albeit a less effective and slightly more philosophically robust type – certainly nothing with the means to solve this particular difficulty for him.

At this point, it was important to remind oneself that ethics were, of course, a Western luxury – a parlour game invented by the European bourgeois, and Simon had a more pressing concern than moral philosophy. Although this, too, was something of an old problem – he didn't have enough money. It had been the single greatest tragedy of his life. It wasn't really as if his demands were extravagant – after all, he was a philosopher and he generally roamed in the realm of ideas rather than the senses. He was certainly no Doug, but there again he was no Diogenes either, and it was going to require more than a barrel, some rags and sunshine for him to get through life. He needed other things – cigarettes and cannabis and decent red wine principally, but also books, and he had to spend at least two months every year in France, otherwise bad things happened to him.

The problem had been more acute than usual. His salary this year had risen by a laughable one point six per cent, but that was to be expected and he had long ago stopped worrying about that. What could he do? He was hardly likely to go on strike about it. He was a professional philosopher and all too aware of how ludicrous that would look. No, the real concern was what had happened with poker night. He had studied Vijay's spreadsheets and, flawed as they were, they confirmed what he had feared – it was becoming less and less profitable. Last year had been a record – what with their monthly sessions and other scratch games he had managed to find, he had made two thousand pounds. And the first half of 2009 had been at least as good, but over the last few months things had dropped off alarmingly. His personal finances, never chaotic but always precarious, couldn't tolerate this going on much longer.

It was Alan who was the problem, and Vijay's spreadsheets showed that. Nick was still quite as hopeless and lucrative as ever, but something troubling had happened to Alan. Somehow or other, and Simon had no idea how it had happened, Alan had got good at poker. Maybe it had something to do with his corrected vision, but he'd started to play properly. His twitching and flinching and folding had come to an end. But poker was a zero-sum game, and if Alan wasn't going to lose any more then someone else would have to. It was either that or Simon would have to win less, and he wasn't going to let that happen. He needed to put a five-hundred-pound deposit down by the end of the month for a little *gîte* in the Dordogne for the next summer, and one way or another someone was going to have to pay for it. If that meant he'd have to use some unorthodox, ethically complex tactics, then so be it.

'Call three pounds,' said Nick.
   'Meet the three, and raise another two pounds,' said Alan.
   'Call,' said Doug.
   'Fold,' said Simon.
Vijay stopped to think for a minute. He felt harassed and put-upon. Nowadays, even Alan would sigh and roll his eyes

while he made his deliberations. What had happened to poker night? He couldn't understand it, it was yet another of those unquantifiable problems, but something seemed to have gone wrong. Why didn't he enjoy it any more? Why had everyone else started behaving so strangely? It wasn't so much that people's manners had got worse, though they had, but they had started *playing* differently.

The spreadsheets could tell him at least part of the story, and he had spent some time going through them. They told him, for instance, that Doug was no longer the player he was. No doubt about it. In 2008, and he knew this without even having to check his records, Doug recorded a positive result on ten of the eleven occasions they had played. He won an average of fifty-four pounds per game, with a standard deviation of just twenty-two. He was the very model of consistency, much more so than Vijay himself or any of the others. Even Nick couldn't lose as consistently as Doug won. But this year, it had been a completely different story. So far, he had won an average of no more than eighteen pounds, but far more alarming was the fact that the rate of variance had now risen to ninety-three! In four years, it was the highest ever recorded.

Vijay suspected there was something sinister going on. It wasn't just that people weren't playing poker in the same way, they weren't even playing for the same *reasons*. He'd detected it before. Something had gone badly wrong with their motivations. They weren't playing for fun, or even to win money. There was something else behind it. Maybe that was why everyone looked so unhappy. He couldn't be sure, it wasn't easily measurable, but hadn't it once been more enjoyable?

It didn't help that they were playing at Simon's. It was his least favourite of all their houses, even worse than Nick's, and Simon was the least generous host that Vijay had ever met. Didn't he have anything else to drink other than wine? Did he ever eat anything other than goat's cheese? And couldn't he afford any light bulbs with a higher wattage? It was so gloomy in here and, once again he didn't seem to have even bothered to tidy the place up for them. It was almost as if he didn't like them being there.

'It's your bet, Vijay – five pounds,' said Doug.

'Yes, I know, sorry. OK – call five pounds,' said Vijay.

What had got into them? And had he made the right decision? The simple answer was that he had no idea. That was what happened when you didn't have enough time to think things through. Were they all just supposed to play poker as badly as Nick?

'I'm in,' said Nick.

Simon dealt the fourth card. It was the two of hearts. Already on the table there was a five of diamonds, a ten of hearts and a jack of clubs. Vijay had the nine and eight of diamonds in his hand.

'I'll check,' said Nick.

'Fifteen pounds,' said Alan.

Around the table, there was a gentle outbreak of sighs and shaking heads. Vijay looked at his old friend gloomily. Alan's betting had been a source of concern for some time. On what possible basis was he making a bet like this? And why was he now playing so recklessly and yet doing so much better? He was starting to think that he didn't really understand how this game worked at all.

So, the situation was this: Vijay had nothing as yet, but he did have a seventeen per cent chance of drawing either a seven or a queen with the last card and thereby making the straight. There was no more than forty-five pounds on the table and it would cost him fifteen pounds to stay in. At three to one, the odds weren't quite good enough. It was tempting, of course, but he had to keep his discipline, he had to keep with the process. The wise thing was to stand down, but he would give it another twenty seconds before telling them – after all, he had a reputation to maintain.

'Fold,' he said at last.

'Call fifteen pounds,' said Doug.

'Fold,' said Nick.

Simon dealt the fifth card. It was the queen of spades – precisely the card he had wanted. Vijay stared at it sadly. Recently, there had been quite a lot of this sort of thing going on.

'I'll bet twenty pounds,' said Alan.

'Fold,' said Doug.

Vijay watched as Alan dragged the pot towards him. He was probably more than a hundred pounds up. Vijay was down at least fifty. There had been nothing wrong with his reasoning, the calculations were relatively simple ones and he still took his time over them, but more often than not these days they tended to lead to the wrong decisions. While Alan increasingly tended to make the right decisions for the wrong reasons. Was it any wonder that for the last two months now, at the end of each evening, he'd taken to lying about his losses on the spreadsheet?

After the evening in the hotel, Nick had assumed that he would never see Sophia again. She hadn't replied to the well-crafted email he'd sent her the next day checking she was OK, but then, unexpectedly, two weeks later, she had come to his evening class. It wasn't like before. She sat at the back this time, she frowned and seemed to listen diligently, but said almost nothing, and she had left the class immediately after it had finished, without giving the slightest acknowledgement that he was anything other than someone who taught her. He had gone through her written assignment – an overview of post-feminist critiques of *Mrs Dalloway*, and it was perfunctory with little ambition or attempt to impress him. If there was one thing he knew about it was internet-based plagiarism and, sure enough, it hadn't taken him long to find the two articles she had almost entirely copied it from. Clearly, whatever they had had together was now over. Just to make sure, and because that morning he had received his credit-card bill, he gave it a C minus.

Well, so much for that. Yes, for a couple of hours he thought they had opened up to each other in an important way, but with her rejection, for that's what it was, had come some much-needed clarity. Whatever Sophia's attractions, and they tended to be exaggerated, she was far too much of a headcase for him to risk his marriage over. He had Janet, and that was fine, that was all he needed. He could now see that the last few months hadn't actually been a mid-life crisis, but they may well have prevented one. He had learnt a few things about the world, he had a better sense of where he fitted in and he'd grown up, a little bit.

And where did that leave Doug? Well, he wasn't sure how much credit he could take for this, he wasn't sure how much he *wanted* to take, but Doug was in a bad way. Looking across at him now, with his stupid oversized head, Nick felt a surge of disgust and pity. He'd had too much to drink of course, that didn't help, but there was none of the usual oikish behaviour and stupid jokes, the overconfident betting, homophobic impersonations and semi-latent aggression. Instead, Doug had bypassed all this and gone straight to the maudlin stage. Sitting in the corner, his head bowed, he could face the world with nothing but acceptance and humility. It was hard to believe that this was the monster who had taken thousands of pounds from him over the last four years, who had hurt him with every weapon at his disposal – with his huge house and cock, with his extravagant generosity, and with his flushes and four of a kinds. But now at last, Doug's reign was coming to an end, and it would only need a little more effort on Nick's part to make sure of it.

If he needed any further proof, one only had to look at what had happened to him. For Nick, as Doug would probably have said in happier times, *was on fire*. He had no idea if he was playing well or not, but he was certainly winning. Every single thing he did – every raise, every risk, every bluff, was working. It was like that night last year when he'd drunk Vijay's whisky, but better – more controlled, clearer, easier to enjoy. It made perfect sense of course. It was just like the second law of thermodynamics, or was it the first? The conservation-of-energy principle – Nick had always known that it was the same with luck. There was no more or less luck in the world than there ever had been, it was just the distribution that changed. Doug had had masses of it for years, but now at last he'd lost it, and his luck had passed on to someone else. It had passed to Nick.

It was eleven o'clock. They were cutting the cards for new seats. Vijay was counting his chips, Simon was smoking a cigarette and Doug was being particularly quiet. Normally he could be relied upon at this point to make some ill-informed remark about the state of the nation, but instead he seemed to be brooding. It was Alan, of all people, who was initiating the discussion, with some personal speculations on how the economic situation was going to impact on the software industry. Everyone was immediately interested. In fact, it seemed that the impending economic recession was the most interesting thing to have ever happened to Reading. Vijay in particular had a stock of high-quality, albeit all rather similar, recession stories that he was keen to share with them and even Simon was listening, as he tended to do when the subject of money came up.

Nick wasn't going to let this one pass. Speaking as casually as possible, but looking closely at Doug all the time, he patiently waited for Vijay to stop talking, and then remarked that things must be particularly difficult for the leisure industry, and that he'd heard from someone, he couldn't remember who, that even Doug's business had got itself into a spot of bother. Doug winced, he gave a little start of surprise and a spasm of pain flickered across his large face. But he said nothing.

Vijay dealt the cards. Nick had a ten of spades and a seven of diamonds. But he was more interested in Doug than in his cards. He had been bracing himself for some kind of outburst, some dog-like snarl of rage, and was careful not to catch his eye. Instead there was nothing. Doug's face had curdled, he had hurriedly taken a large gulp from his wine glass and then sunk back into his chair.

'Two pounds,' said Alan.

'Call,' said Simon.

'Call,' said Doug.

'See the two,' said Nick.

'I'll call,' said Vijay.

The flop was dealt on to the table: the ten of hearts, the nine of spades and queen of hearts. Well, he had a pair of tens – more than enough to keep going. And just for the hell of it, he was going to push things further with Doug as well. Without minding too much if anyone was interested or not, Nick continued to elaborate on the impact of the recession. Economics was a mystery to him – he didn't even know if it was an academic subject that he should despise or respect. He had certainly never *cared* much about it, and his analysis had never gone any further than noticing that his own levels of well-being tended to run directly counter to the country's general business cycle. Still, he wasn't going to worry about any of that now. With tremendous authority, he announced to the group that the era of brainless prosperity was over, the days when any dickhead would call himself an entrepreneur and start printing money with dim-witted schemes were gone, and how relieved Doug must be to have a business managed by people as experienced and sensible as the Lakises.

'Three pounds,' said Alan, who didn't seem to be in the slightest bit interested in what Nick was saying.

'Fold,' said Simon.

'Call,' said Doug, who had now shrivelled up completely into his chair, and didn't seem to be taking part in the game at all.

'Call three pounds,' said Nick.

'Fold,' said Vijay.

Vijay dealt the fourth card. It was the ten of diamonds, which meant Nick had three of a kind. Now that was very useful indeed, and it was almost certain that no one else would have a stronger hand. Of course, a different kind of player, Simon for instance, would now drive the others out; frighten them off with a very large bet, so as to make sure that no one else stayed in and made a flush or a straight with the last card. But Nick wasn't Simon. He knew what he was doing and what the dangers were – he might be a fucking idiot, but he wasn't *stupid*. It was just that he wanted to play a bit more with this hand, and to play a bit more with Doug.

'Three pounds,' said Alan.

'Call three pounds,' said Doug.

'Three pounds, and raise just another three,' said Nick. 'I want to go easy on you all in this new age of economic hardship.'

'I can still afford three pounds,' said Alan.

'Call,' said Doug.

Vijay dealt the final card on to the table. It was the five of diamonds, nothing to worry about. He had got away with it

– just like, not so long ago, Doug would have. Of course, it was still perfectly possible that one of them was holding the two cards they needed for a straight, or even a pair of queens to match the one on the table, but he didn't think that was likely – not unless they had been betting as witlessly as him. No, he had this won, which meant that he could afford to grandstand a little.

'Check,' said Alan.

'Bet twenty pounds,' said Nick. 'And Doug – if you haven't got it, then I'd like you to know that I at least still think your credit is good.'

What an amazingly ugly and spiteful thing to say! Had he completely lost his entire moral framework? He just wished that one day he would be able to explain everything to Doug. He wished he could explain it to himself. But that was enough now. Project Fuck Doug was over and for an obvious reason – Doug was fucked. Poor old Doug. Nick would never have guessed it before, but wasn't he, in some important sense, a victim? Was he anything more than a big-hearted, small-brained man who had got out of his depth – bamboozled by his in-laws, betrayed by the New Economy and manipulated by his more able and pitiless wife? And now, on top of everything else, he was getting thrashed at cards.

'Fold,' said Doug quietly.

'Fold,' said Alan.

Alan looked across at Nick's large and disorderly pile of chips. Ah well, he could hardly mind losing to Nick. In fact, he didn't really mind losing to anyone. Not that he did any more. It was just like all his old self-help books had predicted: as soon as he'd stopped caring, he'd started winning. Of course, what those infuriating things had never done was teach him *how* to stop caring. But no matter, he'd got there in the end. It was funny, though, how little pleasure all this was giving him. He wasn't precisely certain how much he'd actually won in the last few months, and he couldn't be bothered to check Vijay's spreadsheets. Was this the downside of feeling OK about everything – you never got to feel any better than that? Well, if it came down to a choice between mediocrity or misery, it wasn't going to be a very difficult decision. If he ever had any doubts about that, he only had to look at Nick.

As if by way of confirmation, he glanced over at him now. True, he seemed happier than he had all year, but with Nick that could hardly be taken as an encouraging sign. It wasn't as if you'd describe him as *well* or anything. In fact, in many ways, he looked worse than ever. There was something particularly unsettling about him this evening, something dangerous and manic as he cackled and snickered his way to victory. On at least one occasion, Alan had thought he was talking to himself. He was also behaving dreadfully. Again, nothing so very unusual about that, and it was only towards Doug, but tonight Alan thought he could detect a new poise and competency to his spite, as if at long last, along with the poker, it was something he had become good at.

Over the years, Alan had developed a mild camaraderie with Nick. After all, they were the ones that got beaten all the time. But did Alan actually like him? It would be a struggle, surely, to say that Nick was actually *likeable*. And tonight he was already giving an indication of just how frightful he'd be if he did ever become successful. But there was, he supposed, and he wasn't sure if this was the right word, something undeniably majestic about Nick, with his strange powers of misjudgement and purposeless strength of will, his reckless defiance of fortune, his suicidal betting and his incredible inability to ever know when to stop.

Not that the others were in much of a better state. Vijay hadn't been himself for a while, and seemed especially gloomy tonight. But there was no great mystery there – he was losing a lot of money. Well, Alan wasn't going to worry too much about that. OK, technically speaking, Vijay was still probably his best friend, but he hadn't forgiven him for getting him into poker in the first place, and nearly four years of it certainly hadn't done their friendship much good. Maybe poker was a game that brought out the worst in everyone, but there were so many things Vijay did that he now found intolerable: the way he continually counted his chips while they were playing, his need to record and recall all of their wins and losses, the maddening amount of time he took to make a bet, and the fact that every time they played he had to end just a little bit up. Well – it didn't look like that was going to happen tonight.

Anyway, it was Doug that he ought to be concerned about. What on earth had happened to him? It was astonishing to think that this man had once been so fearsome. It was as if he had been put on a course of anti-antidepressants. He was worse than Alan himself ever used to be – fretful and jumpy, but also withdrawn and self-absorbed, unable to look any of them in the eye. Nick was being horrible to him, that couldn't help, but then why didn't he defend himself? At other times, as Alan knew all too well, Doug had retaliated with a terrible force, but tonight he simply flinched and looked sadly away, like a wounded animal. He was drinking too much again, but that couldn't be the problem. Drink didn't usually affect him like this, and he certainly wasn't singing or climbing up the furniture or doing anything amazing, like that night at Nick's which nobody ever talked about. No, tonight was the opposite – the more he drank, the quieter and smaller he became. He hadn't been so very much better last month either. At this rate, he'd be the one who got stuck with a tell. At least there would be some justice in that.

And Simon – what was up with Simon? It was, as ever, impossible to say, but there was something odd about him tonight too. A certain tension he had never seen before – an uneasiness, maybe a slight shiftiness, as if he was worried about something he'd done. He wasn't even playing well. Clearly something was on his mind other than cards. But what else did Simon ever think about other than how to win at poker? Unless, who knows, maybe he had actually been doing some *philosophising*? Was that possible? Was he doing it right now? He'd never shown any signs of it before, but perhaps that's how it worked. He was, after all, the only philosopher Alan had ever known.

Well, one thing was certain – as mad and miserable as they were, none of them had changed as much as Alan himself over the last few months. You only had to stare into his eyes or watch him bluff at poker to see that. Of course, not everything about him had changed – the drugs couldn't make you posh or ironic or anything, and he knew that he'd never be able to size up the others with a sweep of the eyes the way that Simon could, or that Nick sometimes tried. Nor would he ever be able to muster Simon's quiet amusement whenever one of them did something stupid, or bully them like Doug had done by waving his dick about. But increasingly he had found that he could observe their goings on with a kind of calm detachment, a sense that none of this concerned him. What did he care if Doug was unhappy, Nick demented and Simon distracted? OK, he could see it, he could tell it was going on, he could speculate on it if he so wished, but none of it really bothered him.

And tonight, just a few minutes ago as he had played out the hand, there had been something else, a feeling that was, if not entirely new, then one he hadn't experienced for a long time. It had been so novel, so unexpected, that for a while he hadn't been able to place it. But suddenly now he could, and as he did so he found himself gently smiling. He was feeling *bored*.

There was just half an hour to go. Nick was almost two hundred pounds up. Doug, Vijay and even Simon were all down. But this was only the beginning. He'd lost thousands of pounds to this bunch over the years, not to mention the emotional costs, and there was work to be done if he was going to get it all back. He had the king of spades and ace of diamonds in his hand – not bad at all. Vijay dealt the flop on to the table, and down came the jack of spades, two of clubs and ten of hearts. So all he needed now was the queen for a straight with two cards still to come. What were the chances of that happening? One in four? One in ten? Nick could never remember, and anyway, he was hardly going to start worrying about probabilities now.

'Bet three pounds,' said Nick.

'Call,' said Alan.

'OK, call,' said Simon.

'Call,' said Vijay.

'Raise another three,' said Doug.

There was a little round of good-hearted moans as everyone put in another three pounds. Although this was potentially good news. Nick needed a good hand, but he needed someone else to have a good one as well. It was no use everyone folding and him sweeping up the small pots – now that the luck was with him, he had to make the most of it. He had to win big.

'See your three and raise five pounds,' said Nick.

'That's eight to me then – OK, call,' said Alan.

'Call,' said Simon.

'Call,' said Vijay.

'Call,' said Doug.

Vijay dealt the fourth card on to the table, and sure enough, it was the queen of hearts. So he now had the straight. Somehow, he had never doubted for a moment that he wouldn't. That was what being lucky felt like. If you had it, you were never surprised or even especially pleased by it; it was just what you came to expect. It was only the luckless who got thrilled and overexcited when good things happened to them. Nick had it, and that meant he was going to get straights and flushes and full houses and all the other good things in life, and there was no point in getting in a state about it.

'Bet ten pounds,' said Nick.

'Call ten pounds,' said Alan.

'I'll meet your ten pounds, and raise another five. So I gather you've been sharing with Mrs McLain some of the fruits of your cultural expertise?' said Simon, oddly. It wasn't like him to make conversation while they were playing. It wasn't really like him to make conversation at all.

'Fold,' said Vijay.

'Call,' said Doug.

'Call the five. Yes, modern and contemporary literary fiction. Very popular course, every Monday night – you should come along,' said Nick. He had no idea why Simon was asking about this now, it wasn't as if he hadn't bragged about it before. But it certainly didn't do any harm to remind everyone that he wasn't just someone who won at cards, he was also a teacher of men and women, an educator.

'Call,' said Alan.

'That's funny, I'm sure I saw Sophia having her lesson on a Friday. At the Entropy bar, near the university?' he said, and then, just to make it absolutely clear, 'You know the one, not far from where I live.'

Nick looked at Simon in horror. It was like Doug's cock all over again – he felt disorientated, punch-drunk, dizzy with surprise and fear. Now, this was a calamity that he had never foreseen. So they *had* been caught, and by Simon of all people. And trust that fucker to make use of it like this. He wouldn't do anything stupid like blurt it out, but nor would he just do the decent thing and keep his mouth shut. No, he would use it. He wouldn't use it to hurt anyone or make mischief, but he would use it, in a highly efficient and dastardly fashion, to extract all he could from it. What a bastard. Meanwhile, Doug had jolted forwards with a start. It was as if he had been slapped on the cheeks, or had a bucket of iced water thrown over him. The depressed lethargy had abruptly gone, but it hadn't been replaced by any anger. He just looked terrified and bewildered, as if he had woken from a long sleep and found himself in a horrible and unexpected place. Slowly, painfully, his maladapted brain went through its analysis, reinterpreting and adjusting all of the evidence, painfully moving towards the hypothesis that Sophia had been talking to Nick.

Nick stared at Simon, and tried to generate as much hostility as he was able. Concentrating as hard as possible, narrowing his eyes and flaring his nostrils, he attempted to focus a laser beam of distilled rage at Simon's forehead. He managed to hold this for no more than five seconds, before abruptly and implausibly opening his eyes wide, rearranging his face and tilting his head into a puppy-like expression of sorrow and pleading. But neither approach was going to work. He couldn't intimidate Simon and he certainly couldn't make him feel uneasy or guilty, he knew that. For Simon was that most vile of things, a *philosophe*r – which meant that he was a sort of anti-human, a ruthless and macabre analytical machine; not like Vijay who harmlessly calculated company finances and the probability of drawing two pairs, but rather he tried to work out the dimensions of human souls and the purpose of the universe. Maybe he'd picked the wrong monster all those months ago. And to think that, once upon a time, Nick had so wanted Simon to like him.

It was vital that Doug didn't know that he had kissed his wife, however briefly and incompetently. Although not entirely predictable or well understood, the consequences, Nick knew, would be appalling. Doug would be pretty fucked up about it, but he'd also be utterly fucked off. It was almost certain that he'd beat him up, and maybe Sophia too. Christ – *Sophia* would then probably beat him up as well. It would bring nothing but violence and destruction and dishonour upon him, it would probably mean the very end of poker night itself, and the kind of cosmic bloodbath that engulfed and destroyed all participants. Doug might be wrecked, but whatever happened, Nick had to avoid some kind of Greek tragedy – that was the very last thing his life needed right now.

Vijay dealt the last card – the five of clubs. It was now impossible for anyone else to have a stronger hand. There were no pairs on the table, which meant that no one, not Doug, not Simon, not even Alan with his antidepressants, could have a full house or a four of a kind, and there were no more than two of any suit showing, which meant that none of those bastards could make a flush either. It was possible, but highly unlikely, that someone else had a king and ace hidden and so had exactly the same straight as him, but even that didn't change the key point – he couldn't be beaten and so could bet with impunity. Or at least, he would have been able to, if he wasn't now being blackmailed.

Was he bluffing? Would Simon really expose him in this way? Of course, if he did, it's not as if the consequences would be particularly good for any of them. Mutually assured destruction: one of the economics teachers at school had once spent an evening explaining game theory to him, but none of that seemed much help now. It wasn't an issue of optimum strategies or asymmetrical outcomes – the only question of any significance was how big a fucker was Simon? He looked across the table again, trying once more fruitlessly to connect with his blank eyes, and the answer was – quite a pretty big one.

Well, he had to bet something. Alan, the wanker, was tapping the table impatiently, and he couldn't just sit here for ever looking stupid. Not that Doug seemed to have noticed what was going on – that poor sod was now a wreck, stranded in his own dismal little world of self-doubt and hurt and paralysing suspicion and unhappiness. Well, *welcome to the jungle*, as some of his sixth formers liked to say. But Doug wasn't the problem any more. He looked over cautiously to his left. Simon, of course, was staring intently, meaningfully at him. God – was what he was doing to him even *legal*? Fucking hell, they were even round at his house. OK, Simon had never been much of a host at the best of times, but even so – to commit extortion against one of your guests, it was hardly what you'd call hospitable.

'OK, I'll bet ten pounds,' said Nick slowly.

'Call ten,' said Alan. Jesus – never mind Doug, what was Alan still doing here? This was all getting out of hand. There were four of them still in, and the pot now had over three hundred pounds in it – one of the biggest ever, in fact the very biggest if you didn't count the time Doug had been on drugs. But even so, was that really an appropriate amount to blackmail someone for? They might not be friends exactly, but they did at least know each other, they had played cards together for years now, they had a relationship, of sorts – did Simon value it at no more than that? Three thousand pounds would have been more like it, but three *hundred*? Whatever else, he couldn't help but feel that he was being undervalued and disrespected.

'Your ten, and raise another twenty,' said Simon. 'I'm feeling pretty confident that I'm the only one here with the cards that count.'

'Call,' said Doug, although it wasn't at all clear that he knew what he was calling. He was no longer the King of Reading, but King fucking *Lear*. He looked haunted, stupefied with doubt and fear, as if he was grappling with phantoms that no one else could see.

It was Nick's bet and it was time to do something decisive. He might not be prepared to take responsibility for this evening's debacle, but he had to take some control. Pausing for ten seconds or so, he surveyed the table. He looked from one to the other in turn: his old, defeated enemy; the two witnesses who were powerless to help or understand; and finally Simon, the new and far more deadly threat.

'I'll see your twenty and raise fifty pounds,' he said at last, and so loud that he almost shouted it out. It was the most unambiguous bet he had ever made in his life, the clearest possible sign of intent that he could think of – a declaration to Simon to fuck off, to stop being a fucker and to leave him fucking alone, or else they would all get fucked.

'Fold,' said Alan. Well, at least Alan had got the message, even if it hadn't been intended for him.

'OK, I'll see you for fifty,' said Simon. 'I'd be very interested to see how this one turns out, for all of us.'

There was a long pause, while Doug looked sadly around at the others as if for the first time. Poor, simple-minded Doug. Predictably, he had failed to understand the meta-text, and with any luck he never would, but he could sense that something else, something ghastly, was going on. He was shaking his head softly.

'No, I can't do it. Not any more. Fold,' he said, and placing his arms neatly in front of him, he gently put his head down on to the table.

Nick looked directly into Simon's face. No one else mattered. Was he really going to do this to him, to Doug, to all of them? It was time for them to declare their hands, but neither of them was going to rush into this. Still Simon stared back at him. For half a minute all was silent. He'd heard it said that men couldn't communicate like women, or like dolphins for that matter, that they were limited to sound waves at audible frequencies, squiggles on the page and violence. But Nick knew that wasn't true – they had all proved otherwise a thousand times round the poker table. And again, at this precise moment, Simon and Nick were communicating with each other quite as clearly as if they were speaking to one another in English, although no clearer than that.

'So, what have you got?' asked Nick.

'I've only got two pairs – jacks and eights,' said Simon, flipping over his cards. 'But I think that's going to be enough, isn't it, Nick?'

In the end, the final pause was only momentary. Up until then he hadn't been at all sure what he was going to do, but suddenly now there could be no doubt. It was obvious – there wasn't really a choice. Just like his career, his house, his marriage and everything else that mattered, choice didn't come into it.

'Yes, you've got me beaten,' said Nick, his voice shaking as he carefully stacked up his cards and placed them back in the deck. 'I've got nothing. Good call. I thought I was going to get away with it.'

There were gasps of astonishment from round the table. Alan shook his head in bemused wonder and Vijay looked particularly distressed at the sheer reckless stupidity of it all.

There was more than four hundred pounds on the table, it was the most preposterous bluff they had ever seen, and only he and Simon would ever know that the reason he'd been able to bet like that was because it had never been a bluff, he had had the winning hand all along. It was actually Doug who looked the most broken by all this. It was Doug who had folded, whose nerve had failed, and who had been outbluffed by them both. And Nick would never, not even in years to come, be able to tell him that he had been protected from something far worse. He might be stretching it a little to describe his actions this evening as heroic, but with Nick's loss at poker he had saved them both. Not that this was much consolation.

'That was very well played,' said Simon, using both hands to scoop the chips towards him. 'Your bluff very nearly had me. Oh, and you're right – now that I think about it, it was someone else I saw in the pub that night.'

There was a melodramatic cracking sound, as if Simon's table had split down the middle, or else a bomb had just been detonated a mile away in the city centre, or perhaps the universe had juddered to a halt. But it wasn't any of those things. It was Doug, and he had suddenly and unexpectedly let out a great sob of anguish. It was bestial, like the cry of a dying bull elephant echoing across the plains of a starless African night. And it was followed by a dreadful silence.

Nick was in no position to enjoy the sight. For one thing, it was actually incredibly sad. There was no pleasure to be had in watching a man disintegrate, even if it was partly your own doing, and for another he had just been thoroughly buggered by Simon. It was so fucking *unfair*. A whole year of preparation and calculated wickedness, with all that plotting and expense and moral degradation, and after all that his good luck had lasted no longer than one night.

Round at the Black Swan – December

'Call two pounds,' said Vijay.

'Your two and raise three,' said Doug.

It had been Vijay's idea, months ago, to hold the final game of the year at the pub. It was two days before Christmas, but Nick didn't feel especially festive. In fact, looking around, none of them did. And no wonder – what a fucking bunch. Simon had successfully blackmailed him last month, he had spent most of the year trying to wreck Doug's life, Alan clearly wished he was somewhere else, and Vijay was really boring. Is that what friendship was like? God, maybe it was, it wasn't something that he had ever really known much about. This was what was known as camaraderie, this was what adult males did to one another.

He looked at the room glumly. Thank God he was drunk. The landlord had given them their own private room upstairs. It was just like his house – a dark little space, with overvarnished wooden wall panels, mahogany furniture and small iron-framed windows. Again, just like home, the radiator seemed to be broken and was stuck on its highest setting, so the room wasn't cosy but uncomfortably warm, and their faces had all turned an eerie red. They had had a substantial if unsurprising turkey supper with two large jugs of red wine that Simon had refused to drink, and a box of Christmas crackers. Alan's paper hat kept slipping over his balding little head, Doug's had ripped on his big one, and Simon, of course, had never bothered to put his on. Vijay was wearing his, and was still trying gamely to prove that this really had been a good idea. Which was odd, because Christmas wasn't even a holiday for Hindus. Or was he a Sikh? Nick could never remember, he didn't know if he ever had known, and he wasn't at all certain he knew what the difference was anyway.

'Fold,' said Simon.

'Fold,' said Alan.

'Call five pounds,' said Nick.

'Call,' said Vijay.

At least having the game at the pub meant that he didn't have to offer to host, something that would have been especially problematic this month as he was temporarily homeless. For it had turned out that, as well as by Simon, his night in the Entropy with Sophia had been comprehensively observed by two of Janet's colleagues from work, women he had in fact met before on several occasions. It had taken a good six weeks for this to percolate through, and he could well imagine how much they would have enjoyed their earnest and fretful deliberations in the staff canteen and tea rooms as the busybodies and do-gooders of Reading Council Social Services Department gradually mobilised. Eventually a delegation of them had decided to do the decent thing and had come round one evening. And Janet had immediately told him to leave the house. That was two weeks ago, and he had spent his forty-first birthday stranded in a not very friendly, improbably expensive bed and breakfast on the Oxford Road, like a modern-day Robinson Crusoe, without a car or Broadband internet.

Janet wasn't stupid. With hindsight, she may have regretted her choice of husband, but she wasn't going to spend the rest of her life alone. That really would be miserable, and, even if she didn't need someone to look after her, then she certainly needed someone to look after. Besides, in many ways, the marriage worked really well, relatively speaking. It wasn't all *that* dysfunctional: they didn't have violent drunken rows or even get on each other's nerves too much. Neither of them was an alcoholic, or a thief. Nick didn't earn much, but there again, other than poker and drink, he didn't spend all that much either. Nor had it really been such a fatal misdemeanour, and Nick hadn't had to stretch the truth so very much in order to persuade Janet that it had been nothing more than a drunken evening with an overemotional student that had got out of hand but never gone any further. Once they sorted this episode out, they should be able to settle back down to the kind of well-structured calm that had served them so well for the last ten years. In fact, if she hadn't found the sachet of remaining MDMA at the bottom of the biscuit tin, they would probably have already had things sorted.

As it was, he was still negotiating. And, although Janet was going to have him back, it would be at a price. She had lost no time in taking down all of the paintings. Well, maybe that wasn't such a bad thing – he was never going to do it, although there was to be no intermediate stage, in which they lingered in the cupboard under the stairs for six months while he toyed with the idea of getting them reframed. Instead they had already been put in bin bags and taken to the Oxfam shop on Duke Street, where they were currently on sale for two pounds each. Worse still, she had put the ProPokerPlus! on eBay, and already accepted an offer of twenty pounds, or approximately two per cent of what he'd paid for it. Not that he was about to tell her that.

There were other concessions. He had happily agreed to her zero-tolerance ruling on all recreational drugs, but was much less comfortable with the alcohol policy. Could he really be expected to drink less? He was a teacher, and in two weeks the spring term, in some ways the most deadly of them all, was about to start. Her ambitious targets were one of the points they were still to agree on. In addition, Janet had realised that the adult education classes were a long-standing danger and he had agreed that from now on he would come straight home after each class, and that the money earned would go directly into her bank account, to save up for the new kitchen. There had also been a series of protocols around home decorations, visiting her mother and internet use. In fact, just about the only thing she had allowed him to keep unchanged was the poker. Oddly enough, and partly because he had consistently lied about how much money he lost, she didn't seem to mind that so much.

Simon dealt the fifth and final card. It was the seven of diamonds. Already on the table there was a ten of hearts, a five of hearts, an eight of clubs and a king of diamonds. Nick had the seven and eight of spades in his hand, which meant he had two pairs. Two pairs – he'd been playing poker for nearly four years now, and he still didn't know if two pairs was a good hand or not.

'Bet three pounds,' said Vijay.

'Raise ten pounds,' said Doug.

Nick looked over at his stacks of chips. Doug seemed to be having a good time of things, and he was betting like his old self – swift, unpleasant and overaggressive bids that made you feel harassed and uncertain and anxious.

'OK, call thirteen pounds,' said Nick, though he had the familiar feeling that this wasn't going to work out.

'Fold,' said Vijay.

Doug flipped over his cards. He had two pairs as well, but as Nick had suspected, Doug's were better – kings and fives. He dragged the chips towards him. He was beaming, his face flushed with the heat and excitement and pleasure of winning. For some reason, having a bright red face seemed to suit Doug.

Yes, there was no doubt about it – Doug was back to his winning ways. He had made a remarkable recovery, and it seemed that Nick's hugely expensive and hard-fought victory had been a brief one. It wasn't just the way he betted and won, everything about him was a concern. His eyes were sparkling, he was leaning forward, he was alert and adrenalised like an adolescent Labrador. He was all too obviously having a really good time, he'd already made a series of tiresome and vulgar jokes, and now he was about to launch into his Sean Connery impersonation.

Whatever Nick might think, or Sophia come to that, his complete collection of Western literature wasn't just for display purposes. Doug was going to read it all. In fact, he had already started. And he hadn't begun with Jane Austen, but with Homer. The collection may be arranged alphabetically, but he knew better than that. He was going to start at the very beginning and work his way through.

The problem was that after Homer he had immediately hit the tragedies of Sophocles, and after a month he was still no more than a third of the way through *Oedipus Rex*. But he had loved Homer. Most of all, of course, he had loved the heroes. They were like him at his very best – fearless warriors, who tempered their violence with honour and who used their powers to undertake great feats and endeavours. And, just like all of them, he had a fatal weakness too, something that could be exploited by traitors and enemies. He too had an Achilles heel. It was his wife, it was Sophia. Nick had uncovered it.

Even worse, *Sophia* had uncovered it. For the grim truth was that somewhere along the line he had fallen hopelessly in love with his wife, and had been made to pay for it.

How had it happened? When he'd married her it certainly hadn't been his intention. Although never fully discussed, Sophia was meant to have been part of a wider package, one of the many elements in a complex and ambitious deal. Of course, he had taken care to assure himself that she was attractive and in good health and impressive and fertile, but he hadn't bothered to check whether he loved her or not. That hadn't been the point. But the problem was that now he *did* love her.

It was monstrous, and it was pathetic. He loved the way she walked barefoot through the dining room, with her surprisingly large feet slapping against the tiled floor, he was fascinated by her strands of black hair that clogged up the drain in the shower, and the little pools of spilt contact-lens cleaner that she made by the basin in their bedroom. Sometimes, when she looked up from her book, she would catch him looking at her, and would frown, as if irritated by his presence, and he would feel hurt and bewildered and cross, as if he had horribly stubbed his toe against the bathroom door.

He might not know how, but he knew when this had happened easily enough – it had happened at just about the time that she'd stopped loving him. Surely she had once? It was that which had kept him going over the last few weeks. Whatever the circumstances, there must have been something there at the beginning. Surely she couldn't have been as hard-nosed about getting married as he had?

And what was he going to do about it? He was going to get her back again, that's what he was going to do. It was the Doug way. *Ex opus opes* – well, he'd just have to work harder. He'd already started. There was the reading, of course, and he'd already thrown away all of the pornographic magazines months ago. He'd rethought the drinking as well. He wasn't going to stop drinking, rather he was going to *change* what he drank. Less lager and certainly less of the spirits, but red wine was fine, particularly if it was good quality, by which he meant French and not too cheap, and taken over dinner, just like tonight. In short, he was going to be a bit more Mediterranean and a lot less Scottish about things.

He'd also come clean to Sophia, his father-in-law and the rest of the Lakis family about the size of the loan he'd taken on, and one of the cousins was cleverly restructuring the finances. Another cousin was negotiating with the construction company and scaling down the costs of the new health club. You had to hand it to these Lakises. Even Sophia's brother seemed to be making himself useful. They had rethought Doug's role as well. He was going to be less hands-on, not get so bogged down managing the business, and would focus instead on his core strengths: promotion, public relations and sales. They wanted him out of the office, and back out in the centres – meeting the customers, using the machines, going for lunch with suppliers and selling corporate-membership packages.

It made a lot of sense. He was a people person, and dealing with people rather than spreadsheets was what he had always been best at. It was why he was such a good poker player. What was poker, after all, other than marketing? It's why Vijay, for all his calculating, would never be any good. Poker bets and poker pots might be counted in money, but it wasn't a game for accountants. It was a game for people who knew how to sell things. Whether it was a discounted two-year-membership deal to all employees or a pair of kings, it was all about how you sold it. And Doug, once he got going, once he remembered who he was, could sell.

In a way, he had Nick to thank for a lot of this, although of course he was never going to tell him that. It was Nick who had precipitated the crisis. The daft sod had fallen for Sophia, that was obvious. He'd guessed it before she'd even told him. It was exactly the kind of stupid thing he would do. Not that Sophia had been the slightest bit interested, of course, *as if*, but it had certainly made Doug sit up. The idea that that pillock, in his crappy little adult education class in the crappy Further Education College, was strutting his stuff, mouthing off about whatever it was that he was mysteriously paid to know about, to *Sophia*. Well, something had to be done – a response was required. He was after all a sportsman – he needed competition, it brought out the best in him. That's partly why he'd lost touch with the business – without the competition, he'd gone stale.

Not that he'd ever really consider Nick a competitor. He was more like one of those mechanised hares at the greyhound races – a silly piece of nothing that served no purpose other than to get him going. But he had at least done that. Nick had woken him up, made him realise that, if he wanted to have Sophia back the way he wanted, he had to be all the things that he used to be, all the things that Nick could never be. He had to be strong and brave and make decisions. He had to be generous and truthful. He had to respect her family, and listen carefully to what she said. And, above all, he had to be kind. If he had learnt anything, it was that. Just be kind. Not to everyone obviously, but to those that mattered. Otherwise, you got fucked.

Of course, none of this was especially difficult. He'd realised long ago that most of the important things in life, like business and poker, weren't very difficult, you just had to work at them, that's all. Well, he was working hard, and already, in just the last week or so, he'd started to get some results. It shouldn't have come as a surprise. As Arnold Palmer had taught him, *The more I practise, the luckier I get.* Already Sophia was more like her old self around him. She listened to him again and didn't look grumpy when he asked her something, and he no longer felt that she was laughing at him behind his back. No, there was no doubt, the respect was returning. With the respect would come everything else, but in a way even that didn't matter. He loved Sophia, he knew that now, and he didn't even especially need her to love him back. After all, she wasn't going to go anywhere. She just needed to respect his love for her, that was all.

Alan looked at his watch. It was now midnight, but the pub stayed open late, and they had agreed beforehand, on this one occasion, to play for an extra hour. But first there was something that he had to say. For Alan, who above all hated giving speeches, was going to give a speech. Tapping his glass to get their attention, he got to his feet and started. All eyes were on him alone, and would be for the next four minutes, and he didn't mind a bit. It was a testament to how far he'd come in the last few months, a testament to the powers of Western medicine.

First of all he gave them the good news. Alice had just had a three-month scan and they were expecting a baby girl in June. There was an outburst of clapping, well-intentioned cheering and banging on the tables. Vijay and Doug were especially delighted, as Alan knew all parents are when someone else joins their ranks, but Simon was clapping too and even Nick looked pleased, as he too cautiously acknowledged that this was unambiguously something that he shouldn't be unhappy about.

Then he gave them the other, more dramatic news. This would be his last game of poker. He had given it a great deal of thought and decided that, what with getting ready for the baby and everything else, he wasn't going to have the time to play cards any more. He was of course going to miss these evenings enormously, and very much hoped that they kept playing, but it was time for him to pass his place at the table to somebody else.

Of course, this wasn't so well received. Vijay looked as if he might start crying, and Nick looked furious. Well, so what – what did he owe those two anyway? For a long time, it would have worried him, would have stopped him doing this, but not any more. Since when had Nick ever worried about him? If he had any sense, he'd quit too. And Vijay, well, he was a *bit* sorry for Vijay who for some reason loved poker night more than any of them, but he'd still see him. And they wouldn't have to talk about poker spreadsheets any more, they'd be able to talk about other, better things: kids and schools, car-navigation systems, and financial-forecasting software. Unlike the other two, Simon didn't look too bothered. Clearly, now that he wasn't making money from him every month, his leaving wasn't a loss. But oddly, nor did Doug. In fact, if anything, Doug looked a bit relieved.

He sat back down. It was over. He would play for another hour, they would count their chips for the last time, shake hands and then that would be it. His poker-playing days were over, he'd got through it. He'd got through the misery and pain, the curse of the tell, the random hurt and inexplicable sorrow. It had all been part of the course, what went on. It wasn't even the human condition – it was just what happened to organisms on this planet. But it didn't bother Alan any more. He wasn't very good at poker, not really, not like Simon or Doug, but that didn't bother him either. Some hands he won now, and some he still lost. That was fine. Once upon a time he used to think that the point of life was not to get beaten. But he knew better now. The point was not to play – not if you didn't want to. And Alan didn't.

* * *

Nick looked across at Alan with contempt and envy. So the little creep was getting out. In truth, Nick had gone off Alan ever since he'd stopped losing, and he was still cross about the anti-depressants thing, but this was a blow he hadn't expected. And after all he'd tried to do for him – somehow it seemed a bit ungrateful. Of course, Alan had never really seemed to like playing very much, even when he was winning, but for him to just stop playing like this, that was unbelievable. Was he really allowed to do that? Weren't there rules or something?

But there was more to come, because Doug, *Doug*, had now risen unsteadily to his feet and was making a speech as well. It was a less cogent affair all round. Alan had probably been rehearsing his for days, but he suspected that Doug had only now decided to do this. It was far longer, but it amounted to much the same thing. Doug, just like Alan, was retiring from poker. He'd enjoyed it immensely, but enough was enough. He needed to devote more attention to his family and business. He acknowledged that he'd been under a lot of strain for the last few months, he apologised if that had been obvious during their games and reassured them that he had started to take control of his life again. Giving up poker was all part of this. Nick looked at him warily – Jesus, was he having *therapy* or something? Of course, forcing Doug to retire from poker had been the objective all those months ago, but he was meant to have been driven out, not to just fucking leave because he felt like it.

But Doug wasn't finished. For some reason, he now wanted them to know that he was going to spend time on other things, the kind of things that he and Sophia could do together. Things like art collecting, for instance – the painting he'd bought earlier this year had just been valued by a dealer at ten thousand pounds, and while he obviously didn't yet have the expertise and knowledge of some of the others round the table – he was looking at Nick here – he might at least have a good eye, and it was something he'd like to see if he could take further. He thanked them again and, with a final flourish of well-meaning barbarity, he apologised to Nick for having won so much money from him, without giving him the chance to win it back next year. Nick smiled weakly. Right to the end, he still didn't know if Doug was the biggest bastard he'd ever come across in his life, or just the stupidest. And now he never would find out where all that good luck had come from.

So that was it. Poker night was over. Now what was he going to do? Well, he was going to keep playing, that's what. He'd find another game, he'd find some other players. And if no one would play him at poker, then he'd find something else. He'd form a pub-quiz team or take up chess or international socialism. Or perhaps he'd become a trade-union rep and go to war against the school governors or else maybe the other union reps. He wouldn't win of course, and anyway – winning was for losers. But he'd keep playing, he'd keep hurting and being hurt and he would never learn from his mistakes. There were many more pointless disasters, glorious defeats and ruinous victories still to be had, many more monsters and villains to plot against and misjudge, to stand up to and get beaten by. There were all manner of bets and bluffs to make, and all kinds of pots and prizes to compete for, and he would never ever fold. Even when it was the right thing to do, *especially* when it was the right thing to do, he would never fold.

Simon dealt the cards. Nick had the two of clubs and nine of diamonds. Hopeless. But he had never counted on being dealt a good hand, in cards or anything else.

'Bet three pounds,' said Nick.

'Fold,' said Vijay.

'Fold,' said Alan.

'Call,' said Doug.

'Call your three, and raise another five,' said Simon.

Nick looked fiercely across the table at his opponents. He had an hour left to play, at least in this game. He was, he reckoned, about eighty pounds down. But there was still plenty of time to make it all back, which meant there was still time to lose a lot more. He looked down at his dwindling pile of chips in front of him and back up at the others and if, for the merest second, there was a flicker of pity or shame or sadness across any of their faces, then he was too deep in thought to notice.

A NOTE ON THE TYPE

The text of this book is set in Linotype Stempel Garamond, a version of Garamond adapted and first used by the Stempel foundry in 1924. It is one of several versions of Garamond based on the designs of Claude Garamond. It is thought that Garamond based his font on Bembo, cut in 1495 by Francesco Griffo in collaboration with the Italian printer Aldus Manutius. Garamond types were first used in books printed in Paris around 1532. Many of the present-day versions of this type are based on the *Typi Academiae* of Jean Jannon cut in Sedan in 1615.

Claude Garamond was born in Paris in 1480. He learned how to cut type from his father and by the age of fifteen he was able to fashion steel punches the size of a pica with great precision. At the age of sixty he was commissioned by King Francis I to design a Greek alphabet; for this he was given the honourable title of royal type founder. He died in 1561.